"Are You Following Me?"

Lindsay asked as she regarded the handsome stranger next to her. As glad as she was to see him again, there was something decidedly odd about these repeated meetings. Unless she believed in Kismet—which despite her mother's best matchmaking efforts, she most definitely did not— there had to be a rational explanation.

"It seems like the other way around, bright eyes. You got on this plane after I did, remember?"

"Just luck."

"And running into me at the coffee shop?"

"Coincidence," Lindsay said flatly. Either she'd beaten astronomical odds or there was more to this than she knew. She tried to forget all her questions and sit back and relax. But how could she, when a stranger who'd dominated her every thought all evening had suddenly appeared right next to her for the third time in one very long night?

Dear Reader,

Welcome to Silhouette! Our goal is to give you hours of unbeatable reading pleasure, and we hope you'll enjoy each month's six new Silhouette Desires. These sensual, provocative love stories are both believable and compelling—sometimes they're poignant, sometimes humorous, but always enjoyable.

Indulge yourself. Experience all the passion and excitement of falling in love along with our heroine as she meets the irresistible man of her dreams and together they overcome all obstacles in the path to a happy ending.

If this is your first Desire, I hope it'll be the first of many. If you're already a Silhouette Desire reader, thanks for your support! Look for some of your favorite authors in the coming months: Stephanie James, Diana Palmer, Dixie Browning, Ann Major and Doreen Owens Malek, to name just a few.

Happy reading!

Isabel Swift
Senior Editor

SDRL-7/85

SHERRYL WOODS
Come Fly with Me

Silhouette Desire

Published by Silhouette Books New York

America's Publisher of Contemporary Romance

SILHOUETTE BOOKS
300 East 42nd St., New York, N.Y. 10017

Copyright © 1987 by Sherryl Woods

ISBN: 0-373-05345-2

First Silhouette Books printing April 1987

America's Publisher of Contemporary Romance

Printed in the U.S.A.

Books by Sherryl Woods

Silhouette Desire

Not at Eight, Darling #309
Yesterday's Love #329
Come Fly with Me #345

SHERRYL WOODS

lives by the ocean, which provides daily inspiration for
the romance in her soul. Her years as a television critic
taught her about steamy plots and humor. Her years
as a travel editor took her to exotic locations. Her
years as a crummy, weekend tennis player taught her
to stick with what she enjoyed most: writing. What
better way to combine all of that than by writing romantic stories about wonderful heroines, sensitive
heroes and enchanting locations.

To Charlotte, whose friendship
and laughter have made the bad times tolerable
and the good times even better--
wishing you warmth on those cold Denver nights.

One

Lindsay's hand hesitated in midair, right between the candy bars and the more expensive, but sinfully tempting, gold foil bag of chocolate-covered almonds. Guilty emerald-green eyes glanced at the healthy selection of trail mix, raisins and dried sunflower seeds hanging on a nearby rack, then looked longingly back at the candy. For a woman used to making quick decisions, this simple one seemed to be beyond her tonight.

She'd had a perfectly rotten week of nonstop, pointless traveling, a full day of endless, mind-numbing meetings, and to top it off she'd been given this lousy out-of-town, weekend assignment that held all the appeal of being asked to tiptoe over quicksand. She deserved a salary increase for this one, and she'd told Trent Langston just that. She deserved a huge, mind-boggling raise, maybe even a promotion. She certainly deserved the candy.

"Go on," a husky voice, filled with apparent amusement at her indecision, urged in a seductive murmur just over her left shoulder. "Take the candy. In fact, take both of them."

To strengthen the taunt, a very masculine hand, sprinkled with crisply curling dark hairs, picked up the candy bar and the bag of chocolates and dangled them in front of her.

"It's easy for you," she retorted, not taking her eyes off the candy and the blunt, well-manicured fingers holding it. "You're not the one who'll have to diet the rest of the weekend."

A low, disbelieving, sexy-as-hell chuckle greeted the comment.

"It would take more than a little chocolate to ruin a figure like yours," the seductive voice replied boldly.

The sincere and decidedly masculine appreciation in that voice at last drew Lindsay's gaze away from the candy. She looked up into dark eyes that danced with the light of a million twinkling stars, eyes that seemed to caress her, even as they teased. Her breath promptly caught in her throat, and the quick retort she'd planned died on her lips, as her gaze traveled over broad shoulders covered in a soft wool shirt of bright-blue plaid and on to narrow hips emphasized by snug-fitting, well-worn jeans. A soft, unspoken "wow" sizzled through her senses and sent them reeling.

He looked exactly like a blatantly sensual adver-tisement for the rugged outdoors—craggy features that spoke of strength and character and fascinating hard living, straight black hair that gleamed like silk and caressed the collar of his shirt, and a tanned complexion that at this time of year hinted at long hours on the beaches of Hawaii or the ski slopes of the Rockies.

She surveyed his attire again, trying not to notice that the muscular body it covered was sending little laser beams of excitement straight into her. Those clothes—with this man in them—definitely belonged on the ski slopes. With a mountain range behind him and a huge stallion under him, he could lure the most timid female alive into heading directly for the wilderness with a whole knapsack of candy bars on her back. Lindsay, who'd absolutely hated the outdoors until about ten seconds ago, could practically smell the alluring fresh scent of pine and the aroma of coffee brewing over an open fire. If the Colorado scenery were landscaped with more men like this, the weekend might not be quite so bad after all.

Stunned by the impact of his obvious virility on her unusually responsive senses, she drew in a sharp breath, blinked and looked nervously away. Simultaneously she was struck by the oddest sensation that if this incredibly gorgeous man, with his whipcord lean body and intense, discerning eyes, approved of her petite, rounded figure, she certainly had no right to complain or worry about it . . . even if she had always wanted to be a more intimidating, more alluring five-feet-nine with long, sleek legs and a model's slenderness.

Silently she held out her hand for the candy. The almost instinctive gesture was greeted by a lazy, satisfied smile that created dimples deeper than any crater Lindsay had ever seen. She had a feeling women would do extraordinary, otherwise inexplicable things for a glimpse of those dimples.

The man nodded approvingly. He put the candy into her waiting hand with a slow, lingering, electric touch, then winked—incredibly long, dark-as-soot lashes sweeping against tanned skin like the soft fluttering of a bird's wing.

And then he simply walked away. Just like that, in a blink of her eyes, he was gone. Vanished, almost as if she'd conjured him up.

But a lingering scent of cologne proved he'd been no figment of her imagination, and suddenly Lindsay experienced the keenest sense of loss she'd felt in years, a reaction that both confused and puzzled her. They had exchanged only a few intimate glances and even fewer words, and yet she was struck by the onset of a totally unfamiliar loneliness. She was torn between standing in line to buy the chocolate, which she now craved more than ever, and impulsively following the handsome stranger through the airport terminal, as though he were some sort of magical Pied Piper who held the seductive promise of romance in his eyes.

"Ridiculous," she muttered under her breath, decisively forcing her gaze back to the newsstand clerk who was waiting impatiently for her to pay for her purchases: *The Wall Street Journal*, three weekly news and business magazines, one candy bar *and* one bag of chocolate-covered almonds.

As Lindsay walked slowly through the terminal to the departure lounge for her flight from Los Angeles to Denver, she thought about the startling and certainly unexpected impact of that brief encounter. The image of those dancing black eyes taunted her in a way no other man's had. Those laughing eyes had been filled with such intelligence, such intuition and such a teasing promise of simple, old-fashioned fun, the sort she rarely had and repeatedly told herself she didn't miss.

Mentally she shook herself, irritated by her totally irrational, wayward thoughts. This was par for the course in her emotional life. In her work as an attorney for a major entertainment studio, she was surrounded by men with sharp minds and even sharper wits. Many of them were even more handsome than the stranger, in a more sophisticated, polished way. But many of them were also egocentric jerks, children in need of constant attention and a steady stream of unquestioning adulation. Not a one of them had ever sparked the sort of sharp sense of sexual awareness that this rugged stranger had. For just a moment there had been this aching tug, this acute yearning deep inside her, as though her body were encouraging her to make a fated match after twenty-nine years of carefully planned, very successful and well-ordered independence.

Of course, when it finally struck, such lightning bolt attraction had to be toward a man she'd never see again, she thought with a sigh. Definitely par for the course.

"Tabor, you've obviously taken one too many late-night flights," she admonished dryly. "You're suffering from a severe shortage of sleep. Why else would you suddenly want to follow a total stranger to the ends of the earth and back again?"

Perhaps all those coast-to-coast flights had simply robbed her brain of sufficient oxygen to think rationally any longer. Perhaps she would spend the rest of her days responding only to such sensory stimuli as dark-as-midnight eyes and sexy dimples. Not altogether such a bad fate, she thought with a momentary pang of longing. It was certainly better than going off to Denver and chasing around in the snow and cold after some nut, who obviously didn't want to be found. Unfortunately, though, she was being paid to stalk one incredibly elusive, terribly talented David Morrow, not some apparent vagabond in a blue plaid shirt and jeans, whose lean, muscular build and attractively rugged appearance suggested he probably worked on a construction crew or rounded up cattle whenever he was short of cash.

"Too bad," she murmured aloud, before forcing her hands to spread open *The Wall Street Journal.*

She had finished the almonds and was halfway through her candy bar and the front page of the paper, when they announced that her flight had been delayed due to a heavy blanket of fog over Denver.

"Ladies and gentlemen, we are anticipating that Stapleton Airport will open again shortly, and as soon as we have word on the opening, the new departure time will be announced. Please remain in the gate area or check back with the agent in approximately one hour. Thank you and we apologize for the inconvenience.''

Lindsay groaned. Not again. Flight delays were a way of life when you flew as much as she did, but she'd never been able to take them in stride. They only added to her anxiety level and they were especially infuriating on nights like tonight when she didn't want to make the trip in the first place. She was dead tired. She hated cold weather. She abhorred snow. And she absolutely despised being sent after some eccentric man, who liked to hide away in the mountains and who'd already made it perfectly clear that he wasn't interested in any offer her company had to make. He'd canceled every meeting they'd scheduled, and his own agent hadn't been able to talk any sense into him. Why on earth did Trent Langston think she'd have any better luck simply by tackling him on his home turf? If anything, he'd have an even greater advantage there.

"We're wasting our time," she'd protested vehemently to her implacable boss.

"You can change his mind," Trent had assured her. "I have complete confidence in you."

"How am I supposed to change his mind? The man doesn't want more money. You've already offered him every conceivable perk from a chauffeured limousine to twenty-four-hour-a-day champagne and caviar the entire time he's on location, to say nothing of a luxury suite and round-the-clock women—"

"A secretarial service," he corrected dryly.

She'd scowled at him. "Whatever. This contract is ninety-nine percent in his favor. The only thing it doesn't have is probably the one thing he wants: creative control over the movie. If you won't bend on that, I don't seem to have a lot of leverage."

"Smile a lot."

"Right," she'd snapped sarcastically. "I tried that on his agent. The sleaze offered to show me his personal collection of signed Picasso prints...in his suite in Monte Carlo."

"It would have been a nice trip."

"Oh, go to hell."

"I'll go there, if you'll go to Denver." His crystal blue eyes had bored into her. "I want David Morrow to write this screenplay, Lindsay."

Lindsay had bowed to the inevitable. Now she was spending a perfectly good Friday night, when she could have been soaking her exhausted body in a bubble bath up to her chin, sitting at L.A. International, chewing on a candy bar instead of her nails and waiting for the fog to lift in Denver. On nights like this she wished she'd taken a job in a library, instead of going into entertainment law.

Maybe she should have married some nice, down-to-earth wanderer like the alluring stranger with the lazy, heart-tumbling smile, had several rowdy, dark-haired little boys, learned how to bake chocolate chip cookies and joined the PTA. This beguiling image danced briefly in her mind before she shuddered. Not a good idea. In the long run, she'd be better off in Denver, snow or no snow.

With at least an hour to kill, she decided to head for the coffee shop. She might as well sit back, try to relax and kick off the sensible, medium-heeled gray pumps. They were killing her feet after nearly sixteen hours of running around the twenty-story tower of Trent Enterprises and the twenty-five acres of Trent Studios, where Trent Langston, grandson of the founder, reigned like some feudal tyrant. She found an empty booth, sat down and slid her slim, stockinged feet out of her shoes. She'd get the coffee in a minute, just as soon as she surreptitiously massaged her aching feet. With her green eyes closed, she sighed with sheer pleasure. Heaven! Absolute heaven!

"Stand up," an intriguingly familiar voice suddenly ordered softly, as Lindsay's heart instinctively started skittering along in triple time. It couldn't be! Her eyes snapped open. It was.

"Stand up," he said again, giving her another of those lazy, enticing smiles.

"You don't really want me to do that," she replied warningly.

"Why not?"

"Because my feet may fall off and you'll have to carry me all the way to my flight."

He surveyed her from her short, stylishly tousled auburn hair to her coral-tinted toenails, a distance of barely five feet, and grinned. "No problem."

Lindsay shook her head. "Somehow I knew you'd say that," she groaned, still not budging. He probably carried logs heavier than she was just for fun. "Why do you want me to stand up in the first place?"

"To see how much damage the candy did, of course."

She nodded sagely. "Of course."

"You did eat it, didn't you?"

"Almost every bite," she admitted ruefully.

"Almost?"

She held up half the chocolate bar. He grinned. "And?"

"It was worth every calorie."

Dark eyes skimmed over the empty tabletop. "And now you're starving yourself to death?"

She chuckled at the obvious disapproval in his voice. "No. I merely collapsed into the first vacant chair I came to and haven't had the energy to move again. Not even for a cup of coffee."

He nodded and the smile returned. "Stay put. I'll be right back. You take it black?"

Lindsay nodded. She thought briefly about arguing and digging in her purse to at least pay for the coffee, but decided it wasn't worth the effort. Liberation was not only a waste of time, but sheer lunacy at a moment like this. Besides, he didn't strike her as the type to pay one whit of attention to her protests, anyway, now that he'd apparently made up his mind to take her under his wing.

She massaged her feet one last time, then slipped them back into her pumps, afraid that five more minutes of such gloriously comfortable escape would make them swell. If that happened, she'd never get them back into the shoes again. The idea of padding barefoot all the way to her gate brought a tiny, half smile to her full, sensual lips. The thought of being carried to the gate in the stranger's strong, muscular arms set off fireworks in her abdomen. The smile grew broader.

"Something funny?" the man asked, suddenly reappearing and putting a cup of black coffee down in front of her.

Lindsay blushed and shook her head.

"Nothing you want to tell me about," he guessed with a knowing grin as he sat down opposite her with his own cup of coffee, into which he promptly emptied half a dozen sugar packets as her eyes widened and her stomach churned in a sort of horrified disbelief. For a chocoholic she had an amazing aversion to straight sugar.

"Something like that," she said, responding at last to his comment.

"Tell me, do you always spend your Friday nights hanging around airports?"

"Whenever I can," Lindsay retorted dryly. "I like to watch the planes take off."

He glanced around and nodded. "Sounds like fun." He paused. "Could I make just one tiny suggestion, though?"

"Certainly."

"You might have a better view if you sat near a window."

"Gee, I'd never thought of that."

"Are you sure you don't just come out here to see if you can find some handsome stranger who'll whisk you away to an exotic location for the weekend?"

"Now that's an intriguing idea," she said thoughtfully. She gave him a dazzling smile. "Going anywhere interesting?"

He returned the smile. "Home."

"Care to take me along?"

He surveyed her slowly, dark eyes burning into her very soul. "Now that really is an intriguing idea," he said softly, leaving the words to whisper along her spine like a gentle, intimate caress.

Lindsay's heart slammed against her ribs. Suddenly the innocent game had turned serious and she couldn't figure out when the rules had changed. One minute they'd been teasing and the next they were... what? Still teasing, she told herself sternly. What else could it be? Strangers did not pick each other up in airports and fly home together. Her gaze lifted to meet the dark-eyed stare that hadn't wavered one tiny bit. On second thought...

"You're not drinking your coffee," he said quietly.

Lindsay picked up the cup absentmindedly, her hand shaking so badly she nearly spilled it. If he laughs, I'll throw it in his face, she thought furiously. He had no right to get to her like this. She gave herself a mental shake. It was hardly his fault that her brain had turned into mush back at the candy counter. Maybe there'd been something weird in the chocolate. Nope. It had happened long before she'd taken the first bite. It had happened when he'd first looked into her eyes, when she'd first seen those devastating dimples.

"Don't you have a flight to catch?" she asked hopefully. This encounter had probably gone on long enough. She was getting more of those funny little feelings in the pit of her stomach, and now they had nothing to do with his excessive use of sugar.

"Not right away. We have plenty of time to catch up on old times."

"Old times?" she echoed weakly. She'd obviously spent too much time with staid corporate types, who talked about rational things like production figures, bottom lines and industry trends. She was having trouble following this man's train of thought.

"It's been nearly an hour. What have you been doing with yourself?"

Lindsay blinked and looked at him to see if there was the slightest sign that his mental breakdown was as complete as hers seemed to be. Was that something you should be able to see by looking into a person's eyes? She stared into his. They looked perfectly normal...dark and intriguingly dangerous, clear as a bell and interested. Very interested. She gulped.

"Have you missed me?" he asked with an impish grin.

"Hardly." Well, now, she admitted to herself, that was not exactly true. He hadn't been far from her thoughts for the past hour or more. It was hardly something to confess, however.

He looked hurt and she felt the strangest need to apologize.

"I'm sorry," she heard herself saying, then added, "Have you missed me?" Even after the perfectly ridiculous question was out of her mouth, she couldn't believe she was actually waiting breathlessly for his answer.

"Terribly," he said solemnly.

Lindsay started to chuckle at the man's outrageousness, but then her gaze met his...and held. Her heart skittered crazily again. The man was lethal. Definitely lethal. Or she'd been bored beyond reason waiting for this dumb flight.

Or maybe she'd just been bored lately by her life.

That nagging possibility crept in so unexpectedly, it took her breath away. She gazed back into speculative eyes, then looked away. At the untouched coffee. At the steady line of customers surveying the coffee shop's array of salads and sandwiches. At her watch. Suddenly her eyes widened in dismay.

"Oh, my. I've got to run. My flight...I have to check on it. Thanks for the coffee," she added, holding out her hand. It was only polite, she told herself. It had nothing to do with the fact that she wanted to touch him, to see if those strong fingers of his were as warm as she remembered. They were. Warm as a sunbeam and a thousand times as stimulating. Electric tingles went racing along her spine.

"You're welcome, bright eyes," he said softly, releasing her hand only after several impossibly long seconds.

Freed from his touch, Lindsay ran, forcing herself to concentrate on her need to catch this damnable flight to Denver, rather than the confusing feelings about the all-too-fleeting touch that had turned her blood to warm honey.

"Hey," he shouted after her, halting her in midstep as she raced along the concourse. When she looked back, he grinned and gave her another one of those lazy, enticing winks that tumbled her heart straight down to her toes. "We'll have dessert another time."

She reached the gate just in time to hear the announcement that the flight to Denver had been canceled. She wanted to pound her fist into something and, quite possibly, to scream. Very loudly. Instead, frazzled nerves and all, she waited dutifully in line to find a booking on another flight.

While she was waiting, she realized that she still had no idea who her intriguing, mysterious stranger might be. Bumping into him once was sheer, heart-thumping good luck. Crossing paths with him again had been incredible, blood-sizzling coincidence. But the odds against her ever seeing him again must be astronomical. No, she decided sadly, there would be no dessert.

But, she thought as a soft smile tilted her lips, the main course had been the stuff of fantasies.

Two

What do you mean you can't get me another flight tonight?'' Lindsay snapped irritably at the harried clerk behind the ticket counter, then winced at her unreasonable tone.

Just because she was exhausted and frustrated beyond belief was no excuse for taking it out on this poor woman, whose eyes seemed to be glazing over at the prospect of dealing with the long line of equally frustrated, nasty-tempered people behind Lindsay. She did not envy the ticket agent the hours she'd spend trying to satisfy all of these people who'd planned to spend a nice, relaxing weekend skiing, not standing around in an airport battling for seat space. At least she'd been near the front of the line. If anyone got a seat, she would, but the outlook appeared dim and much as she hated the whole idea of this trip, she was doomed to make it. She wanted to get it over with tonight, not tomorrow.

She took a deep, calming breath. "I have to be in Denver before morning on business," she explained in a more civilized tone. "Please. You have to get me on the next flight."

"I'm sorry, Miss Tabor," the flustered agent said, punching frantically at the computer keys as though that might make a seat materialize. "There's only one more scheduled flight for later tonight and there's not a single coach seat left on it."

"What about first class?" Lindsay asked with a sigh.

She'd always resisted the temptation to buy first-class tickets, especially on these shorter trips. It seemed an absolute waste of the company's money, even though Langston Studios could probably afford to buy its own airlines. But tonight was an emergency created specifically by Trent Langston! That alone was motivation enough to buy a first-class ticket.

On top of that, she deserved a little pampering for a change. This was her fifth flight this week, and considering how she felt about flying in the first place, it felt more like her fiftieth. It was nearly midnight already. She hadn't slept soundly in her own bed for days, and the last decent meal she'd had—or almost had—was in a perfectly delightful Italian restaurant in New York five days ago with David Morrow's awful, knee-squeezing agent, Morrie Samuels. She'd been so busy planning defensive maneuvers against his roving hands, she hadn't eaten more than a few bites of the delicious angel's hair pasta primavera. Since then, she'd been living on stale sandwiches and coffee. And—she smiled ruefully—on candy bars.

The thought of the candy reminded her of her mystery man and a little spark of pleasure soared through her. When the clerk looked up from the computer at last, Lindsay's tired grumpiness had virtually vanished. She gave the girl a beaming smile. "Well?"

"There's one seat left in first class," she announced, her voice filled with relief.

"I'll take it." Aside from the pampering, it would give her a chance to test her mother's theory that she could meet the successful, handsome man of her dreams, if she'd only fly first class during the hundreds of flights she took each year on studio business.

"The kind of intelligent, successful man you need is not about to spend three hours with his knees under his chin and someone else's kids drooling over his shoulder," her mother had told her repeatedly.

Marie Tabor had flatly ignored Lindsay's constant denials that she even wanted a man in her life—in the air or on the ground. Pursing her lips stubbornly and glaring at her equally stubborn daughter, she had continued, "He's going to want to sit back and relax with a nice meal, maybe some champagne. And then he'll want enough room to spread out all those contracts for big, lucrative deals. If you're not interested in him, think about those deals. At least business seems to turn you on."

"If the man's doing all that business, he'll never even notice me," Lindsay had retorted.

"Of course he will. You're a beautiful woman. Not that you do anything to make the most of it. You're always wearing those drab, tailored suits that look so alike I can't tell one from the other. And your hair..." She shook her head sorrowfully. "It's so lovely. Couldn't you think about getting it cut in a style that's a little less..." She waved her hands helplessly. "A little less...unusual? It looks like it's been whipped with an eggbeater."

Lindsay had grinned at the plaintive note in her mother's voice. Her dark auburn hair was short, tousled and casual. It took her exactly ten minutes to wash it and another ten to blow it dry. It suited her fast-paced lifestyle.

"I was thinking of dying it pink next time," she teased. "What do you think?"

"Don't be absurd!"

"That's no more absurd than your idea that buying a first-class ticket will also buy me love."

"Just try it. For me."

Lindsay sighed. Well, tonight she was trying it. Her mother would be thrilled. She had half a mind to make a quick stop at a pay phone to let her know. She glanced at her watch and groaned.

"Forget it. I'll call her from Denver and tell her about the engagement," she muttered under her breath, as she picked up her carry-on luggage and ran down the concourse, barely making the jetway before the door slammed closed. Breathlessly she entered the plane, stowed her luggage and slid into her seat. She fumbled with the safety belt, but one side steadfastly refused to budge from between the seats. Still short-tempered, she was about to stand up and yank the blasted thing loose, when a hand gently nudged hers out of the way and a familiar voice drawled softly, "Don't kill the thing. It just needs a little gentle persuasion."

Lindsay's eyebrows shot up and her eyes widened as she twisted in her seat to stare into very familiar black eyes.

"Exactly like a woman," he added seductively, those bold, laughing eyes never leaving hers as his hands stilled, a mere hairsbreadth from her thigh. Her muscles tightened better than they ever had at the gym.

Trying to hide the sudden trembling of her hands by clenching them tightly together in her lap, she managed a wobbly grin. "And I suppose you know all about women?"

"Enough," he said succinctly, as he snapped the seat belt together, his hands innocently grazing her thighs and sending not-nearly-so-innocent heat waves roaring through her. "About as much as I know about seat belts."

Suddenly Lindsay regarded him suspiciously. As glad as she was to see him again, there was something decidedly odd about these repeated meetings. Unless she believed in Kismet, which she most definitely did not, there had to be a rational explanation.

"Are you following me?" she demanded, eyeing him cautiously. She'd thought she'd read this script just last week....

He chuckled. "Hey, bright eyes, you got on this plane after I did, remember?"

That, at least, was true enough. But a good spy or thief or whatever would have a logical explanation ready, wouldn't he? "What about that meeting in the newsstand?"

"Just luck."

"And the coffee shop?"

"Coincidence," he said, echoing her earlier analysis. Somehow it didn't seem as convincing coming from him. Not when he was sitting beside her yet again, dimples firmly in place as though they'd been etched in stone by a smitten female sculptor with an eye for very seductive masculine features. Either she'd beaten the astronomical odds or there was more to this than she knew, and she'd never beaten the odds before in her life.

"Exactly why are you here?" she inquired suspiciously.

A mischievous grin tugged at his lips. "I'm flying to Denver," he said very seriously.

She moaned at her stupidity. It would be difficult to argue with that. She rephrased the question. "Why are you going to Denver?"

"I told you earlier. I'm going home...to Boulder," he said with perfect aplomb. Then, giving her a wicked smile, he taunted, "What are you doing on this flight? Are you following me?"

"Of course not," she sputtered indignantly. If that wasn't the most ridiculous, egotistical suggestion... even though the thought had crossed her mind once or twice.

"Hey, simmer down," he soothed, chuckling again. The low, throaty sound rippled over her. "You asked first. Don't I get a turn?"

Lindsay grunted. After her cross-examination, she supposed he should have his own shot at it, but the question had sounded so absurd when he said it. She tried to put her faith in her legal training, in her instinctive ability to size people up instantly. She studied the firm set of his jaw, the crinkling laugh lines that gave his face life and character, the dark hair that edged over the collar of his blue plaid shirt and the dimples that came with a taunting smile. She found absolutely nothing that seemed the least bit threatening...unless you counted the fact that the whole of all those parts had sent her pulse rate tripping along in the danger zone.

She tried to forget all of her questions and doubts, to sit back and relax, but it was impossible. There wasn't a woman alive who could relax when a stranger who'd begun dominating her every thought suddenly appeared right next to her for the third time in one very long night. If she weren't careful, she *was* going to start believing in Kismet. As for her mother, she probably owed her one for this. It remained to be seen whether she'd take her out to dinner or break her arm.

"You seem a little tense."

At the sound of his voice and his all-too-accurate assessment, Lindsay jumped as nervously as she had the first time an Italian had pinched her in Rome as she walked unsuspectingly down the Via Veneto. Her gaze flew to the man seated next to her. He was chuckling at her reaction but politely trying to hide it.

"I'm not the least bit tense," she announced stoutly, though the throb of the starting engines had just registered in her mind, setting off another of those waves of anxiety she'd never been able to conquer.

"Then do you suppose you could relax your grip before your fingers fall off?"

Lindsay followed the direction of his gaze and realized that her hands were still clenched tightly in her lap. He was right. Her knuckles were white, though her fingers hadn't quite turned blue yet. They usually did before the plane was airborne. As far as she was concerned, for takeoff she was relaxed.

"You aren't one of those nervous flyers, are you?" he asked anxiously.

"As much as I fly?" she retorted dryly, refusing to concede the truth and expose her vulnerability. She tried to force her hands to separate and lie perfectly still in some semblance of a relaxed pose. It might fool her seat-mate, though it would never fool a psychiatrist. Flying sent her nerves into an absolute frenzy, but she knew if she ever admitted it aloud, she might very well never leave the ground again.

She tried for a confident grin and added brightly, "If I got scared every time I took off, they'd have locked me up in a padded cell by now." What she didn't say was that the cell never seemed very far away, especially now when the plane started taxiing down the runway.

The quizzical expression in his eyes hinted that he wasn't quite sure whether to believe her. "Then what's the problem? Surely you aren't afraid of me."

Actually all of these coincidental encounters were adding to her normal preflight jitters, but she wasn't afraid of him. Not exactly. It was just the way he made her feel... like a teenager falling in love for the first time right after hearing about the birds and the bees. It made her palms itch. However, she was a sophisticated woman. She handled multi-million-dollar negotiations without blinking her eyes. She was not about to discuss her itching palms, her wobbly knees or the flames in her abdomen. Instead, she retorted, "Hardly. It's just been a very long, very frustrating day."

"Ahhh," he said softly and she shot him a puzzled glance. "That explains the candy overdose."

She grinned. It explained some of it at least, the only part that needed explaining. She had no intention of getting into a discussion about how a pair of dark-as-onyx eyes had convinced her she needed to buy up half the candy counter.

"Why don't you tell me about it?" he suggested. "I'd like to know what it takes to drive a beautiful lady to try to overdose on chocolate."

Lindsay shook her head firmly, but the look in those dark, intense eyes was magical. It transported her out of her ordinary, career-oriented existence, away from her fear of flying, into some other world, a world where romance was not only possible, but very likely indeed. Her skin glowed as though it had been brushed by fire, rosy cheeks against white satin. Her bright emerald-green eyes sparkled like precious jewels against a velvet backdrop. And suddenly, for the first time in a very long time, Lindsay felt beautiful, desirable—all from the look in some stranger's eyes. It was a heady, almost frightening sensation. For the third time in just a few hours, she had the feeling she would follow this man anywhere.

"Hey," he said softly. "I thought you were going to tell me about your rotten day."

She smiled back at him and admitted honestly, "It doesn't seem so rotten now." Even more astounding, she had actually missed the precise moment when the plane left the ground. The man was a miracle worker.

He nodded with satisfaction. "Good. Then we can talk about other things. Like who you are and why it's taken me all my life to meet you."

"You've probably been looking in all the wrong places," she told him dryly.

"Obviously. I avoid airports like the plague."

"I don't spend all my time in airports."

"Then where should I have been looking?"

"Oh, here, there and everywhere."

He shook his head. "Not precise enough," he said with feigned sorrow. "By the time I look all those places, we may both be old and have gray hair and wrinkles down to our knees."

"I don't suppose you could love me anyway, under those conditions," Lindsay teased right back, absolutely amazed at the crazy, daring words that seemed to be coming out of her mouth tonight.

He studied her closely. "Well...maybe. With those eyes, I think I could overlook almost anything. Now tell me all about yourself. Then we can tell our grandchildren we fell in love high in a midnight sky, surrounded by stars."

Lindsay blinked, sighed softly and fell a little bit in love right then. The men she knew did not whisper romantic, poetic phrases in her ears, not at 30,000 feet in the air. They talked contracts and megabucks and videocassette rights. The way her pulse was dancing along right now, she had a feeling contract discussions were a whole lot safer. More boring maybe, but safer.

"Maybe we should start by talking about you," she suggested with a little catch in her voice.

He shook his head stubbornly. "You first. Then maybe I'll know what it'll take to keep the sparkle in your eyes and the laughter on your lips."

She sighed again and wondered if the man had a bit of Irish blarney in him. What did it matter? If the man wanted to do that for her, she had absolutely no choice but to comply. You did not turn down offers that came along once in a lifetime, even if you knew they were only good for the length of one flight to Denver.

"Deal," Lindsay agreed soberly, though her head felt anything but sober. She felt as though she were floating away on a cloud of champagne, although the flight attendant had only just now put a glass of the golden, bubbly, intoxicating liquid in front of her.

"Deal," he confirmed, holding out his hand. Lindsay put her hand in his and suddenly, inexplicably felt safer than she had since those long-ago nights when her father had picked her up, swung her high in the air and then held her tightly the minute he'd come home from work.

Until she was nine.

Until he'd died.

Since then she'd felt she had to keep running, to fill her life with lots of places, lots of people, none of whom ever got too close. Even as a child, she'd been afraid, though her fears had been vague, unformed. As she'd grown older, the fears had been more easily recognizable. She'd been afraid to be alone with her thoughts. Afraid of her growing desires for companionship. Afraid of commitment. Afraid of losing someone she loved. She'd even kept an emotional distance between herself and her mother, always preparing herself for the inevitable day when her mother would leave her too.

Lindsay looked again into the stranger's eyes, felt the warmth of his firm hand holding hers, the security hinted at by the touch and knew instinctively that the running might very well be over. She also knew she wouldn't stop without a fight. She'd been at it far too long and grown far too good at it.

Even now, however, she couldn't talk about herself, despite the deal they'd just made.

"You first," she urged again. "Who are you?"

He was clearly puzzled by her reluctance to open up, but he relented.

"Okay, if you insist. I'm Mark Channing. I live just outside of Boulder, in a small, cozy house with a spectacular view of the mountains, and not a soul around to spoil the quiet," he said in a soft-as-silk, bedtime-story voice. Lindsay settled back in her seat and let the sound wash over her, replacing the low roar of the engines, lulling her into a wonderfully soothing, near-hypnotic trance.

"The pine trees stand out dark and bold against the white backdrop of snow this time of year. In the spring pink and purple and white wildflowers pop up everywhere. The world looks as though it's been covered with a crazy-quilt of color."

The deep voice throbbed with passionate excitement as he talked about this special wonderland, yet Lindsay couldn't help feeling a certain amount of dismay. It sounded so horribly lonely.

"You must feel very isolated," she suggested tentatively.

"Only if I choose to be. There are some terrific people who live nearby and I'm not that far from town. I go in at least once a week for supplies. I try to meet some friends for dinner, maybe take in a movie and then go back. Usually I can hardly wait to get home," he confessed, with a rueful half smile.

"Do you do a lot of traveling?" she asked hopefully.

"Not if I can help it. Not anymore, anyway," he added almost as an afterthought. "The last couple of weeks have been an exception. I had to go into Los Angeles to see a producer, then to New York to straighten out some business problems and then back to L.A. to try to get out of a ridiculous contract I'd told my agent not to negotiate in the first place. With any luck I won't have to leave Boulder again for the next six months. Maybe more. I don't want to miss summer."

Lindsay grew increasingly uneasy as he talked. His comments seemed to strike an all-too-responsive chord. Surely he was not the elusive author she'd been sent out here to track down and seduce by whatever means possible into signing a deal. The contracts in her briefcase were for David Morrow, not Mark Channing. But exactly how many men from the Denver area could possibly be playing cat and mouse with a movie studio at precisely the same moment?

"What do you do?" she asked with what she hoped was no more than casual interest.

He grinned at her in a way that gave her the distinct impression that she'd committed some sort of social gaffe. "I write a little."

"Books?"

"Usually," he said cryptically.

"What else?"

"I've done a couple of screenplays."

"Under your own name?"

"Yes."

Lindsay breathed a sigh of relief. It wasn't the same man after all. Thank goodness. Mark Channing was taking enough of a toll on her senses without throwing in the electricity of a volatile contract negotiation.

"What have you done?" she asked.

He sighed, as though the question were all too commonplace and bored him to tears. He ticked off several titles, including an Academy Award winner, as Lindsay's relief turned to dismay all over again.

"But you said your name was Mark Channing," she muttered accusingly.

He looked puzzled. "It is."

"Those films were written by David Morrow."

"That's right," he agreed easily. "David Mark Channing Morrow. I stick with the middle names in my private life. It's easier."

"Oh my God!" Lindsay moaned, burying her face in her hands. She'd forgotten all about those stupid, double initials—M.C.—in the middle of the man's name. So much for magic and romance. She was about to start talking megabucks at 30,000 feet after all.

"What's wrong?"

She looked at him and tried for a sunny, dazzling smile. It wavered. "It appears I am following you, after all," she announced.

"You're what?"

"Well, Mr. Channing or Mr. Morrow or whatever your name is, it seems I'm on my way to Denver with an excellent contract for you from Trent Studios," Lindsay explained with practiced confidence, trying to ignore the little white lines of annoyance that suddenly edged his mouth. He looked as though he might be about to let loose with an angry roar. She tried to forestall it with another smile.

"Quite a coincidence, isn't it?" she said cheerfully.

He glared back at her, the twinkle in his eye gone, the dimples vanished. She missed those dimples like crazy. Aside from being sexy, they'd been reassuring. There was nothing reassuring about his current expression. He looked like an angry thundercloud about to dump a flood on a world with which it was greatly displeased.

"It really is a coincidence," she swore solemnly, holding up her hand.

Finally, his stormy expression wavered, then softened. And then he was chuckling.

Lindsay stared at him indignantly. "What's so amusing?"

"You."

"Me?"

He nodded, then laughed again, shaking his head. "You're quite a surprise."

"Why?"

"My agent's description did not exactly do you justice, Ms. Tabor."

At least he knew her name. Morrie'd probably taken it in vain in very graphic words her mother would wash her mouth out with soap for using. Lindsay waited expectantly for him to say more...about the contract, about his agent, about her. Nothing. "Well," she prodded at last. "What did Morrie have to say?"

Mark threw up his hands. "If you insist. Let me try to recall it exactly. He said you were, and I quote, 'more aggressive than a damned Doberman. If she's got a heart, it must be made of iron and her mind's like a damned steel trap.' He threw in a few other, more colorful adjectives, but I'm sure you get the drift."

He looked over at her, his eyes twinkling again. "I gathered that you must have turned down his advances. Morrie doesn't take rejection well."

Lindsay's mouth had settled into a grim line. "I told him to take a flying leap off the George Washington Bridge."

"That must have crushed him."

"I don't think a steamroller could crush him."

He chuckled. "In the long run, you're probably right. Defeat never lasts more than a minute or two with Morrie. That's why he's such a good agent. He really liked you, you know. He told me I was being a stubborn, damned fool for not sitting down and talking to you about this contract. He said you were just my type."

Lindsay was confused. "But you said..."

"I said his description didn't do you justice. He didn't say a thing about those bright green eyes of yours." A finger reached out to gently outline the curve of her cheek, just below her eye. Lindsay felt her skin grow warm, responsive.

"Or the way your lips curve into a sexy pout when you're thinking. Or the shimmering silk of your hair." A handful of short, dark auburn curls ran between his fingers, as his eyes captured hers, teasing her with their mischievous twinkle. "Or the fact that you're hardly bigger than a kitten I could hold in the palm of my hand."

His voice was soft and husky with sensuality. It washed over Lindsay in soothing, enrapturing waves. She tried to snap herself out of the hypnotic spell he'd cast over her again. This wouldn't do. Not at all. She was supposed to get this man to sign a contract and she had no intention of doing it by tumbling into bed with him. And if she didn't get a grip on herself she hadn't a doubt in her mind that bed was exactly where they were headed. Unlike old Morrie, the sleaze, this man clearly could wrap her around his finger—or do far more, if he chose—with a single little come-hither glance.

She tried to revive every ounce of her irritation when he'd failed to show up for their previously scheduled meetings. She'd spent a frustrating extra two days in New York, days that she didn't have to spare, waiting for his promised arrival, only to learn he'd gone back to L.A. She'd trailed after him, only to discover that he was already heading back home.

Instead of being angry at thinking of all that, Lindsay suddenly started chuckling. She couldn't help it. Glancing sideways at him, she noticed that his lips were twitching as well.

"Interesting how fate has accomplished what Morrie and Trent Langston were unable to do," she noted dryly. "They both tend to believe they're omnipotent."

"I was just thinking the same thing." He shook his head ruefully. "If I'd only known."

"What would you have done? Skipped the coffee?"

"I think, Ms. Tabor," he said, his tone suddenly quite serious, "I might very well have bought you the best dinner you've ever had in an airport."

His seemingly innocuous words hung in the air between them and Lindsay's heart skipped one beat and then another as she tried to interpret if there were any hidden meanings behind his remark, whether they were entirely personal or whether there was anything to suggest that he might listen to reason about making a deal with Trent Studios after all. Ironically, at this precise moment, she wasn't at all sure which interpretation she preferred. She decided to stick to business for the moment. It made her less nervous.

"Would you have signed the contract?"

He shook his head slowly. "No," he said flatly, killing her rising hopes. "I'm not interested in the deal. I've told Morrie that. I've told your boss that. Now I'm telling you that."

"I thought you were just bargaining for creative control over the movie."

"Would you give it to me?"

"No. It's the one thing Trent will never give up."

"Don't look so defeated. It doesn't matter. That wouldn't have done it anyway. In fact, there's not a thing in the world that will change my mind."

"Then what did you mean . . ."

"When I said I wouldn't have given you such a run for your money?"

"Yes."

"I meant, Ms. Tabor," he told her in a low, husky tone that sent an anticipatory quiver shooting through her spine, "that I'd have met with you a whole lot sooner, if I'd had any idea what a lovely, intriguing woman you were." His eyes met hers and held. "But I'd have done it for one reason and one reason only."

Lindsay couldn't tear her eyes away from his. "What's that?" she asked in a little choked whisper.

"To get to know you better."

Three

Once Lindsay's heartbeat slowed to its normal rate, she groaned in frustration. She felt like screeching in a decidedly unladylike way or punching her fist into the thick padding on her seat . . . or, better yet, slapping David Mark Channing Morrow's smilingly complacent, handsome face, which was once again displaying his dimples to full, charming advantage. He obviously had big hopes for the two of them. For that matter, so did she. Or anyway, she had.

Three hours ago, back in the newsstand, or even fifteen minutes ago, she might have given anything to hear those sexy, complimentary, seductive words tripping off this man's tongue. Now she'd have been a whole lot happier if he'd said something thoroughly boring and businesslike, such as, "Where do I sign?"

Then he could have told her how beautiful she was and how much he wanted to get to know her and it would have sounded like sheer heaven. Instead, Trent Langston's edict that she come back with David Morrow's signature on a movie deal put something of a damper on her purely feminine response to the sultry look in his eyes and the suggestive tone in his voice.

Which, come to think of it, might be just as well.

Still, she glowered at him. "Do you mean to tell me that I'm on a flight in the middle of the night into some godforsaken, snow-bound place and I'm wasting my time?" she raged, not quite sure why the confirmation of what she'd known before she ever walked out of Trent Studios should upset her so much now.

The man next to her grinned infuriatingly. "Oh, I don't see this as a waste of time at all. We can spend the next few days getting to know each other at Trent Langston's expense."

"I do not use my expense account to wine and dine lost causes," she snapped indignantly. It was beginning to seem that David Morrow was exactly as she'd imagined him after a week of this ridiculous cross-country hide-and-seek: a nut, a jerk, another obnoxious, immature, egocentric, macho... She ran out of adequate words to depict her rapidly sinking opinion of the thoroughly despicable rogue next to her. She was even more irritated by the fact that her still-skittering pulse had not seemed to register just how much of a louse the man obviously was.

"Then we'll use Morrie's," he said with perfect aplomb. "He dragged us into this. It'll do him good to spend a little money for a change."

She gazed at him in astonishment. "You think it's amusing, don't you?"

"Amusing?" he repeated doubtfully, then shook his head. "Not really." He smiled lazily and those devastating dimples deepened. She'd never have believed that was possible. "I just think it has endless possibilities. Don't you?"

Lindsay looked into his steady, interested gaze and blinked. When he looked at her like that, he didn't seem like a jerk at all. He seemed incredibly alluring, downright sexy. She sighed. When he sent those little sparks tripping over her nerves, the weekend certainly did have possibilities—none of them good for her state of mind and every one of them almost impossible to resist. She clenched her hands together in her lap again and resisted like crazy.

Pretend he's Morrie, she told herself sternly. That ought to do it.

She glanced out of the corner of her eye. Impossible! They might have some sort of odd-couple business relationship, but this man was definitely no Morrie. Morrie Samuels had beady little eyes, sweaty hands and slick lines that had made her skin crawl. This man was something else entirely and, while he made her nervous as hell, he definitely did not make her skin crawl. He made her tingle from head to toe and that was intriguing but very dangerous.

Well, resist anyway, a little voice muttered back. She did the best she could.

"I do not!" she said adamantly, noting proudly that there was only a slight squeak in her voice. "You must be out of your mind if you think I'm going to hang around Denver for no good reason.'' She shuddered. ''It's cold there. Record lows, in fact.''

''I live in Boulder.''

''Unless there's a fluke in weather systems which the National Weather Service and I are both unfamiliar with, it's just as cold there.''

''I have a fireplace.''

''I'll just bet you do,'' she muttered under her breath. ''And probably a cozy sheepskin rug in front of it.''

''As a matter of fact—''

''Forget it. I'm spending what's left of this night in a hotel room in Denver and then I'm taking the first flight out in the morning.''

''And what exactly do you plan to tell your boss on Monday?''

''That you weren't interested in a deal, which is just what I told him this afternoon and what, according to you, he has been told several times in the past. It shouldn't come as a big surprise.''

His expression was speculative. ''I've heard a lot about Trent Langston. Do you honestly think he'll be satisfied with that excuse?''

''It's not an excuse. It's the truth.'' She shot him a murderous glance. ''Oh, hell. Of course, he won't be satisfied with it. He'll think I blew it somehow, but,'' she added stoutly, ''that's just too damn bad. If he wants you, he can come out here and try to brainwash you himself.''

''You're willing to give up, just like that?'' Mark said curiously.

"I am not giving up just like that," she snapped back. "It's not as though this is our first offer."

"It's *your* first offer."

"What exactly is that supposed to mean?"

"Why don't you stick around and find out?"

"Because I'm not a masochist."

"But from everything Morrie said, I thought you were ambitious."

"Morrie's judgment is not exactly top of the line," she countered coldly, then added wearily, "Look, obviously, I'd rather go home with your signature on a contract, but you've made it very clear that you don't even want to hear what I have to say. You've certainly gone to extraordinary lengths to avoid me. You must have your own reasons for distrusting Trent Studios and nothing I'm likely to say is going to change that." She hesitated briefly and regarded him with a mix of hope and curiosity. "Is it?"

"No."

"I thought so," she said with a sigh. "Then what's the use of my hanging around for a couple of days and then still going home with an unsigned contract?"

He smiled brightly. "You can tell Trent Langston you tried harder."

"He'll be thrilled," she retorted sarcastically. "And what do you get out of all this? The chance to watch me squirm?"

"No. Like I said before, I just get the chance to get to know you."

The concept completely baffled her. He didn't trust her employers, which meant he couldn't think too highly of her, either, since in his mind she was inextricably bound together with Trent Studios. And yet he wanted to know her better. Lindsay knew she was reasonably attractive, but so were half the women on this plane, and unlike her they were all going willingly to Denver to frolic in the snow. No, it still didn't make sense.

"Why do you want to?"

He shook his head. "I thought I'd made that clear. I must be losing my touch." He gazed straight into her eyes, dark sincerity matching wits with flashing skepticism. "I've always wanted to fall in love under a midnight sky with someone with bright green eyes."

She tilted her head and studied him closely. He actually seemed to mean it. "You're crazy."

He shrugged. "I'm a writer. It goes with the territory. Now are you coming home with me or not?"

Home with him? Now that was another intriguingly dangerous thought, a thought not even to be considered. "I am going to a hotel room," she said firmly. "For the night ... or what's left of it."

"And then?"

Lindsay sighed. He was right about one thing, if she flew home first thing tomorrow morning, *this morning,* Trent would never believe she'd given this her best shot and he'd spend three solid weeks castigating her. She'd either have to slink around the studio on tiptoes and look apologetic or hide out someplace until his temper cooled down. Neither of these alternatives appealed to her. She liked to work, not cower around in the shadows while Trent went into one of his notorious sulks like some overgrown brat.

"I'll think about it," she said.

"Good," he said, nodding in satisfaction, as the plane glided down on the runway. "I'll pick you up in time for breakfast."

When the pounding started on Lindsay's hotel room door, she was convinced it was all part of a sadistic nightmare. She'd barely gotten to sleep under the thick down comforter that hugged her body with a delicious warmth. She poked one finger out from under the covers and tugged at the comforter until she could peek out.

A pale sliver of weak sunlight filtered through a crack between the drawn drapes. It didn't look as though it had a very good grasp on the day. She sighed and snuggled back into the warm nest she'd created for herself. Surely no sane person would be out at this hour of the morning. It must be a mistake.

The pounding started again and an all-too-familiar voice called out her name.

She groaned and buried her face in the pillow. She'd been right. It wasn't a sane person. It was David Mark et cetera. How could a man who'd gotten off the same plane that she had only a few short hours ago be on her doorstep at this hour? He either had a terrific metabolism that didn't require sleep or a sadistic streak a mile long. She suspected that anyone who willingly lived where he had to dig his car out of snow drifts on a regular basis was sadistic, masochistic and probably all sorts of other disturbed things as well. He probably belonged in an institution that treated such disorders. He definitely did not belong in her hotel room. Not at this hour.

"Out of bed, bright eyes," a husky voice called to her, then added hopefully, "Unless you'd like me to come on in and join you."

Another interesting thought, her muddled mind said, mulling it over before her rational side noted that he was already turning the handle of the door. Her eyes widening with shock, she realized that the knob was not only turning, but the door was opening. One size-eleven foot, clad in a cowboy boot, stepped onto blue carpeting leaving disgusting little droplets of melting snow. By the time the rest of Mark Channing—she was going to have to get used to calling him that—followed, she was kneeling in bed, the comforter clutched tightly around her, her eyes flashing dangerous sparks.

"What the hell do you think you're doing?" she demanded in as ferocious a voice as she could manage after being awakened from a sound sleep by a madman. She sounded a little like a pesky Chihuahua, all snap and very little muscle.

"Picking you up for breakfast," he said calmly, black eyes drifting appreciatively over her bare shoulders and down, lingering at the spot on her surprisingly ample chest where the comforter was just barely keeping her decent. "I thought you'd be ready by now."

"By now?" she repeated incredulously. "It's the middle of the night."

"It's nearly nine o'clock. If you sleep much longer, I'll have to take you to lunch, and we won't have nearly enough time for skiing."

Lindsay's gaze flew to the sickly stream of daylight, then back to Mark. She glared at him accusingly. "That's all the strength your sun out here can muster up at nine in the morning?"

"It's clear and brighter in the mountains. You should have seen the sky at daybreak," he enthused. "It was all grays and pinks and oranges. It would have made a great painting."

"Daybreak?" Her voice took on a decided squeak. Suddenly the rest of Mark's words began to register. With something akin to horror, Lindsay began to shake her head.

"No," she said firmly. "No mountains! No skiing!"

"But it's beautiful. And skiing is fun. You're going to love it."

"I won't love it." She snapped out each word emphatically.

"We'll talk about it over breakfast."

"There's nothing to talk about."

He nodded. "We'll see," he said soothingly. "Now you get dressed and I'll help you pack your things."

"Pack my things?" She did not want his masculine, ruggedly virile hands sifting through her silky, intimate clothing. It was indecent. Besides, why the devil did her things need to be packed in the first place?

"I'm perfectly capable of packing my own things, when I am ready to leave this hotel and go back to Los Angeles."

"Of course you are—" he said in a placating tone that set her teeth on edge "—when the time comes. In the meantime, I thought it would make more sense for you to stay out at my place. The drive back and forth is hell when the roads are covered with ice.''

Moving out to his place over any kind of roads, Lindsay thought, would be like tossing herself into a pit of vipers. She'd decided that much on the plane last night and nothing had happened since then to make her change her mind. In fact, his virtually breaking into her room just now only confirmed it.

''I think this room will be just fine,'' she informed him politely. ''Other than a staff that seems to give out keys rather capriciously, this hotel seems to have all the amenities I need.''

''Unfortunately, you've already checked out,'' he told her, grinning complacently.

''I've what!'' The tiny squeak in her voice rose to a decided shriek that she knew from past experience was a sure sign that her temper was about to cross over into a rage that few people ever wanted to experience more than once. She tried her best to save it for very special, incredibly infuriating situations involving people she hoped like hell never to see again. This was rapidly approaching one of those situations.

''Well, I knew how you felt about wasting your company's money,'' he said innocently. ''Just last night you were telling me you didn't like to use your expense account on lost causes. I knew right then that you certainly wouldn't expect Trent Langston to pay for a fancy hotel room in the city, while you went off to the mountains skiing.''

''I am not going skiing!''

By now she had a feeling that where she was really going was crazy, stark, raving bonkers. She was kneeling on a bed in her own hotel room, wrapped in a comforter, screeching like a banshee at a virtual stranger who'd broken in and now wanted to pack her bags and cart her off to play in the snow. It might make a decent screenplay, a perfectly hysterical comedy, in fact. It made a lousy morning.

"Oh, Lindsay," he said sorrowfully. "You need to put some fun in your life, some adventure."

"Fun is going for a walk on the beach in eighty-degree weather. Fun is visiting the Louvre to see the Mona Lisa. Fun is having a drink at the top of the World Trade Center at midnight. Fun might even be dancing until dawn at a disco in London or riding a camel across the Sahara," she informed him haughtily, then added, "There is nothing involving snow and temperatures that barely creep over zero and winds that howl like wolves that could possibly be considered fun."

He shook his head. "I can see I have my work cut out for me."

"It's not your job to make me like cold weather. If, for some insane reason, you thought it was, consider yourself fired."

He studied her slyly. "Want to consider a deal then?"

Lindsay understood all about deals. You did not make them with men who were looking at you the way Mark was looking at her right now, as though she were a tasty morsel of prime beef and he'd been starving for a week. However, she'd been well schooled by Trent. You listened to everybody. *Then* you said no.

"What deal?" she asked cautiously.

"You come to Boulder with me. Let me show you what life can be like here."

"And?" she said skeptically.

"I'll listen to what you have to say about the contract."

"That's blackmail!"

"That's a deal," he corrected.

She supposed by his standards, it probably was. She looked at the lukewarm sliver of gray light peeking between the drapes and thought longingly of the sun-dappled beach at Malibu. She'd been promising herself she'd take up wind-surfing and this probably would have been the perfect weekend for it. There would have been lovely, warm breezes, bright blue, cloudless skies . . .

"It's a lousy deal," she grumbled.

He grinned. "It's the only one you're getting."

Lindsay sighed. "Maybe you should reconsider and go to work for Trent Langston after all," she muttered. "You're two of a kind."

"I take it you're coming," he said happily.

"I don't seem to have a choice."

"Well, that's not exactly true. You do have a choice."

"I think it falls into that depressing, gray area between murder and suicide."

He watched her and waited, her words simply hanging in the air like drifting, aimless balloons. Finally, she sighed.

"Oh, all right. Pack my damn bag. I'll be ready in a few minutes."

She hugged the comforter tightly around her and marched into the bathroom as haughtily as she could. She had a feeling the effect was not quite as regal as she might have liked. Worse, with Mark's dark-eyed gaze seeming to burn into her, she had a horrible suspicion she'd left her backside in plain view. It would be incredibly difficult to maintain the upper hand with a man who'd seen you fully exposed.

She slammed the bathroom door shut behind her. Who was she kidding? She hadn't had the upper hand for the past twenty-four hours and giving David Mark Channing Morrow a glimpse of her bare anatomy couldn't possibly make things any worse than they already were.

She glared at the door. If that man thought for one single second that she was his for the taking, then he was in for one mighty rude awakening. He might make her heart pound a little faster than usual and her nerves might be a little more easily rattled, but he also infuriated her. Lindsay knew anger was a very good weapon to use when someone was trying to get under your skin . . . or into your bed. After a few days under the same roof, he'd discover that she might have a smile like the warmth of a summer sun, but she could be colder than a Denver morning if she wanted to be.

The difficult part was going to be adjusting the temperature just enough to get his name on that contract before she froze him out of her life.

Four

When they walked into the still-crowded hotel coffee shop twenty minutes later, the young, attractive, brunette hostess blatantly surveyed Mark from head to toe. He was wearing what Lindsay had decided after two encounters must be his standard man-of-the-wilderness uniform—snug-fitting jeans, wool plaid shirt and impressive, hand-tooled boots. Despite the casual outfit, he looked exactly like some sort of westernized Greek god just descended from Mount Olympus. The hostess nervously grabbed her entire supply of menus in her rush to accommodate him with what Lindsay knew would be the best table in the room.

She did all that before he smiled.

Once he'd given her one of his heart-tumbling, dimpled grins, the poor woman practically fainted dead away. Lindsay had a feeling the bewitched hostess never even noticed her as she trailed along in her prim little suit like some docile, royal retainer who'd been trained to stay ten paces behind.

"I have a wonderful table right back here," the hostess gushed with a fairly dazzling smile of her own. She started toward a large, comfortable table in the back of the room, her slim hips swaying provocatively.

If Lindsay had been the jealous type or, for that matter, if she'd even had any claim to Mark at all, the woman's clear invitation would have made her madder than hell. As it was, she thought she knew exactly how the woman felt. Mark had the same impact on her. His mere physical presence provoked a purely feminine response in her that she was astounded at and not the least bit thrilled about having.

Before they could reach the table the hostess had chosen, Mark stopped and gestured instead toward a much smaller table for two.

"How about that one?"

When Lindsay and the other woman both looked at him oddly, he shrugged and said innocently, "It's by the window."

"Not a smart move," Lindsay retorted. "I'll be able to see all the people slipping around on the ice."

"They've cleared the sidewalks," he countered reasonably.

She glared at him. "There are still little flakes of white stuff coming down and you'll never convince me someone's scattering rose petals. Besides, every time somebody says something out there the words freeze in midair. Have you ever thought about what happens to all those words when it thaws?''

Mark just shook his head and it wasn't until they were seated that Lindsay realized he didn't give a hoot about the weather, the view or their impact on her already-dismayed psyche. He'd had another strategy entirely in mind. It was not the least bit innocent or subtle: the table he'd chosen was so tiny that their knees were bumping, rubbing together in an intimacy that provoked an instantaneous response inside her, just as he'd known it would. Unless Lindsay twisted around until her feet were poking out in the aisle, she was stuck with the little curls of heat that wound their way from their touching knees right straight to her abdomen. She thought about making the quickest escape possible, then glanced outside at the swirling snow and shivered.

Damn Trent Langston! And Mark Channing! She was not going out in that horrendous, subhuman weather. She didn't even own any boots, for crying out loud. She was staying right here as long as she possibly could. She'd figure out a way to ignore those damnably enticing knees brushing against hers if it killed her.

She concentrated on the menu with a certain amount of desperation as she tried to figure out what would take the longest to prepare and even longer to eat. Normally, if she ate at all in the morning, she grabbed a quick danish and coffee at the office and ate while she read through a stack of contracts on her desk, but today she ordered eggs Benedict, a side order of hash-browned potatoes, a large orange juice and a large pot of tea.

Mark's dark brows lifted over eyes that were glittering with tolerant amusement. Okay, she thought. So it's not the order of a five-foot-one woman who'd worried only twelve hours earlier about the calories in some candy. She caught that insufferable, knowing gleam in his eyes and defiantly asked for a side order of bacon as well.

"I'll have the same, except for the tea. I'd like coffee. Lots of it," he said calmly, as the bored waitress made her notations without blinking an eye. She probably assumed they were honeymooners who hadn't left their suite in three days and were bordering on starvation. The intriguingly seductive idea set off another round of fireworks in the pit of Lindsay's stomach. It was a reaction that didn't bear too much scrutiny.

While they waited for breakfast to arrive, they maintained what, for her at least, was a decidedly awkward silence. Lindsay was never at her best in the morning, anyway. She liked to ease into the day as quietly as possible, preferably after a minimum of eight hours of restful sleep. Not only had she tossed and turned most of the night, this man had awakened her several hours before she was even likely to start thinking about being at her best. He, on the other hand, seemed not only well rested, but perfectly content to just sit and stare at her, which made her gulp and look around for something interesting to focus on.

Unfortunately, she finally decided that, like it or not, Mark Channing was the most interesting thing in the room. She met his dark-eyed gaze and her insides melted, even as she again gave herself a staunch lecture on willpower, backbone and resistance. It didn't work any better today than it had on the plane.

When the food finally came—and not a moment too soon—Lindsay's lips quivered in amusement. Just looking at the over-burdened tray reminded her of one of those comedy acts at the circus, when a seemingly impossible number of clowns all climbed out of one very tiny car.

The waitress studied the tray and the table with a practiced eye. In a single smooth motion, she removed the small vase of fresh flowers and the ashtray from their table and plopped them on the next table, dumped the bacon on the plates with the eggs Benedict, moved the orange juice glasses and the cups closer together and then squeezed in the plates of potatoes. They teetered slightly, but with grim-faced determination she maneuvered them in by another fraction of an inch. Lindsay didn't have a doubt in the world that everything would stay right where she put it.

"I'll be back with more coffee in a minute," the waitress muttered, eyeing Mark's empty cup. She might have the ritualized personality of an efficiency expert, but she clearly knew her business. She also knew enough not to make wisecracks about the odd eating habits of her customers. Wisecracks cut into tips.

"I'm starved," Mark said, digging into his breakfast like a lumberjack with a hard day ahead. Lindsay toyed with hers.

"Great juice," he noted. "Fresh squeezed. You can tell."

"Umm."

"Have you tried the hash-browns? They put in a little bit of onion."

"Great."

"Lindsay, your eggs Benedict will get cold if you don't eat it. You're going to need all your energy for this afternoon. Besides, I thought you were hungry."

She was nibbling on a strip of bacon. "I am," she swore solemnly. "I'm just a slow eater." She offered him a dazzling smile that she hoped would convince him that she could hardly wait to get to all this awful food she'd managed to pile up in front of her. She took another sip of her juice. A very small sip.

When she glanced across the table, she noted that Mark was more than halfway through his entire breakfast and wasn't even slowing down. Talk, Lindsay, she instructed herself. If you want to drag this out, you have to get the man to talk, not eat. He is a fascinating enigma, after all, and admit it or not, you do want to know more about him.

No, she quickly corrected. You *need* to know more about him in your professional capacity and that's all! Now's your chance. Think of it as research.

Her gaze drifted outside and she shuddered. Think of it as salvation.

"So," she said with only slightly feigned curiosity. "What made you decide to live in Boulder? Were you born in this area?"

He shook his head and polished off the eggs.

She tried again. "Have you lived here long?"

"Five, almost six years," he said and finished his last strip of bacon.

"Where are you from originally?"

He swallowed the last sip of his orange juice and gestured toward her glass. She sighed resignedly and nodded. He drank the last of that, then said, "New York."

Lindsay was thankful she wasn't an investigative reporter hell-bent on a juicy, extensive exposé. This man was less responsive than the Statue of Liberty. At least *she* had a prepared speech about the tired, the poor and the hungry masses yearning to be free.

Right now, Lindsay could identify with some of those immigrants to whom that speech was addressed. She wasn't poor and she certainly wasn't hungry, but at the moment she was tired as hell and very definitely yearning to be free of this very determined man seated across from her before he dragged her out into that awful weather. With a sort of horrified sense of wonder, she noted that the cold had actually frozen the condensation on the inside of the coffee shop's plate-glass window into little streams of ice that glittered in the sunlight. She ran her finger along one of the icy rivulets and shivered. It was a shiver that went straight through her bones.

Mark watched the gesture and asked suddenly, "What is this thing you have about snow?"

Lindsay tried to think of some way to explain. Nothing she could think of made much sense. "It's just so...cold."

His eyes lit up, warming her. It was not quite enough to compensate for the weather, but it was a terrific try. "Not if you're sitting in front of a cozy fire with a snifter of brandy."

"But that's not what you have in mind, is it? You're determined to take me skiing."

"Skiing is invigorating, Lindsay. You're going to love it. And the fire feels even better after you've been out in the fresh mountain air."

She eyed him skeptically with very reluctant green eyes.

"You'll see," he promised.

With a sudden flash of inspiration, she said, "But I don't have the right clothes for skiing." That was certainly true enough. She'd brought an extra suit, one sweater and a couple of silk blouses.

"So I noticed," he said dryly. "What on earth were you thinking of when you packed?"

"I was thinking that I was going on a business trip," she retorted sourly. "How was I to know that I'd be conducting my business in the middle of a snow drift?"

"Well, never mind," he soothed. "We'll take care of that. I'll take you shopping."

He surveyed the table and noted that she'd barely touched her food. One dark eyebrow arched quizzically and she quickly lifted a forkful of hash-browns to her lips in a futile effort to prolong the pretense. It didn't fool him for a minute.

"You don't really want the rest of that, do you?" he said quietly.

She shook her head guiltily and thought of all the starving people in Africa. Her mother would be horrified at the waste. *She* was horrified at the waste.

"Then why did you order it?"

Before she could answer, he added, "Forget it. I know exactly what you were thinking."

"You're a mind reader now?"

"No. You're just painfully transparent." He sighed and leaned toward her. A finger tilted her chin up so he could look directly into her eyes. "Stop fighting me. We're going to Boulder and we're going to go skiing. I want to share that experience with you for the first time. I want to share a lot of things with you. You're only postponing the inevitable."

Lindsay regarded him plaintively. "What I'm still trying to figure out is how it became inevitable. Why do you want to do this?"

"Ask the gods."

"I was thinking of calling Trent. Or maybe a psychologist."

"They won't have the answer. Not on this one."

She studied Mark curiously. He was lounging back lazily on his chair now as though it were designed for his personal comfort. It irritated the dickens out of her that he was perfectly at ease, while she still felt like some fluttery teenager who'd stumbled into something that was thoroughly enticing but far beyond her experience. He appeared totally confident, sure of himself and, for that matter, of her. The latter puzzled her. How could he be so certain about all of this, when she hadn't the vaguest idea what was happening between the two of them?

"I asked you something last night and again a minute ago, but you still haven't given me a straight answer," she said at last. "Why are you doing this?"

"Having breakfast?" he asked innocently.

"Don't be cute," she retorted. "Why are you practically kidnapping me? You're an attractive man—"

"Thank you."

She glared at him. "You're intelligent. Maybe a little crazy, but that turns a lot of women on. I'm sure there are any number of sexy, attractive, available women who'd be thrilled to pieces if you invited them to spend a weekend secluded in your mountain hideaway."

"I don't want them."

"Why not?" she asked, trying to keep an edge of desperation out of her voice.

He shrugged, but there was a soft light in his eyes as he said gently, "If I had the answer to that one, it might scare us both to death."

Lindsay's expression grew even more puzzled. "Then you're not sure?"

"Nope," he admitted.

"But you seem so confident. It's as though you're in on a secret and haven't told me."

"I think the gods are the only ones in on the secret at this point. I only know that some instinct tells me I shouldn't let you get away."

"Do you always trust your instincts?"

He hesitated for a moment and Lindsay saw all sorts of emotions race across his face. "I do now," he said quietly.

There was something in the way he said those three words, so solemnly and with such great sadness, that touched Lindsay's heart. "Didn't you always?"

"No. Once I was too caught up in my writing to pay any attention to my instincts."

"And something happened?"

"Something happened," he said tersely, his eyes growing cold. She could sense him withdrawing into some distant time and place and knew it was the end of the discussion even before he turned and called to the waitress for the check.

As they drove out of Denver, Mark kept up a running commentary on the scenery, much of which was veiled by a hazy fog. But as they neared Boulder, the fog lifted and Lindsay could see the snow-covered mountains rising majestically like a scenic designer's well-executed backdrop for the town huddled at the bottom. It was picturesque, truly impressive, in fact. She could appreciate it aesthetically. She'd just prefer to appreciate it on a postcard or from a very long distance . . . say 500 miles or so south.

They headed straight for a shopping mall and by midafternoon, ignoring Lindsay's protests that it was a waste of money to be buying clothes for a once-in-a-lifetime ski trip, Mark had her in a shop being fitted for boots, cross-country skis, a wonderfully warm down jacket with matching pants, jeans, another sweater, color-coordinated knit cap and mittens, and long underwear.

Lindsay held up the thick, thermal underwear and regarded it with disgust. "This is the most hideous, unfeminine excuse for lingerie I've ever seen."

Mark's eyes gleamed wickedly. "Do you want to be warm or sexy?"

"Both. I can do that in Los Angeles."

"You're in Boulder."

"A mistake I'm still trying to figure out how I made."

"You couldn't resist my offer?" he suggested, giving her a bold wink. The sales clerk practically swooned at Mark's feet. It was apparently a reaction he was used to, because he didn't even seem to notice it. Lindsay glowered at him and thought of suggesting that he take the obviously infatuated clerk skiing with him. But there was the contract and she still had a little glimmer of hope that she could get him to sign it, if she played along with him for just a while. If she had to stand around in the snow for a few hours, she could do it. She'd hate it, but she could do it.

"Good point," she replied, then inquired brightly, "When are we going to start talking about the contract?"

"Soon."

"How soon?"

"Before you go back to L.A."

Lindsay's eyes lit up. "There's a flight tonight."

"Not that soon. Go try on the clothes."

The jeans and sweater were no problem, but when she came out of the dressing room a few minutes later in the ski clothes, she had a scowl on her face. There was a strange light, a gleam of approval in Mark's eyes and he was grinning at her. He tugged the cap down until it covered her ears.

"I look like an overstuffed sausage," she grumbled.

"You look cute, the perfect snow bunny."

"You have a distorted mind."

"It helps when you're writing," he said, then turned to the sales clerk. "We'll take everything."

Before Lindsay could blink, he'd paid for the purchase in cash and whisked her out the door.

"Is Morrie paying for this?" she asked hopefully. It would serve him right. The things had cost a fortune, maybe not as much as a trip to Monte Carlo, but there were far fewer strings attached . . . she hoped.

"Nope. It's a present from me."

"I don't want any presents from you." Especially not clothing that was suitable only for slightly daft individuals who thought slipping and sliding around outdoors with a wind-chill factor below zero was great sport.

"Don't be ungrateful. It's not becoming."

"It's no less becoming than this ridiculous outfit."

"Tell the truth," he demanded. "Weren't you warmer when we came out to the car?"

"Yes. I suppose so."

"Then the clothes are serving their purpose. I consider it money well spent."

Lindsay shrugged. "It's your money."

"Exactly."

"I don't see why we couldn't just sit in front of the fire this afternoon and drink hot chocolate. Maybe fix some popcorn."

The idea held a certain romantic appeal that she didn't care to analyze too closely.

"Later," he promised, twisting around to gaze at her huddled against the door of the car. The look in his eyes offered far more intriguing possibilities than hot chocolate and popcorn.

"We've got a whole weekend ahead of us. We'll get around to everything, bright eyes." He smiled at her lazily and those dimples set her heartbeat fluttering crazily again. "All in good time."

Lindsay suddenly decided a good romp in the snow was exactly what she needed. It would encase her heart in ice again. Despite the blasts of wind that had frozen her ears and the snow that had chilled her toes, her damn heart had been thawing all afternoon.

Five

_____

Once they had left the edge of town, it took nearly another hour to reach Mark's house. By Lindsay's standards that put it in an isolated wilderness, albeit a Christmas-card-perfect setting complete with snow-covered pine trees and rolling fields that bore not a single footprint to mar the pristine beauty. The silence there was overpowering, and she knew enough about writers to understand why the utter peacefulness of the location might appeal to Mark. She also knew herself well enough to realize that it was going to be all she could do to keep from going stir-crazy in such an environment even with the intriguing, infuriating Mark Channing to keep her company.

With Mark clearly anxious to get her onto skis before she could rally a satisfactory defense, she barely had time to glance around the interior of the house, which was all stone and glass and rough-hewn wood. It seemed to blend right into the natural setting, as though it had been put there by God's hand, not man's. The floors were covered with lovely, hand-woven Indian carpets, except in front of the fire-place, where there was a huge, oddly lumpy sheep-skin rug.

To Lindsay's utter astonishment, the rug rippled a bit like the surface of a pond, then staggered to its feet. The largest, shaggiest dog she had ever seen mean-dered over to Mark, wagged its tail once and licked his hand in a sort of low-key welcome that brought an immediate smile to her lips.

"Shadow, this is Lindsay," Mark said as the dog cocked its head and looked at her. At least she thought he was looking at her. His dark, button eyes were shaded by a thick fringe of shaggy fur.

She held out her hand and Shadow sniffed it po-litely, then, bored with his effort to greet the new-comers, wandered back toward the fire and flopped down again, obviously no longer interested in their presence in what was clearly his domain.

"You leave him here alone?" she asked incredu-lously, adding dryly, "Does he cook his own meals and build his own fires?"

Mark grinned. "Of course not. Mrs. Tynan looks after him. She brought him back up here today. She lit the fire and probably stocked the refrigerator as well, if I know her. When I stopped by to see her this morning on my way to pick you up, I told her I was bringing a lovely guest back with me."

"Is Mrs. Tynan your housekeeper?"

"Hardly. You'll meet her. She runs the general store about a mile from here. She's a crusty old gal, who talks like she could bite nails in two, but she's got a heart a mile wide."

There was a warm note in Mark's voice that suggested Mrs. Tynan was someone very special to him. But Lindsay knew something about small, tight-knit environments. Gossip ran rampant and, if an efficiency expert had done a flow diagram of its path, it would have led right back to someplace like a general store. The idea did not exactly cheer her. This visit was awkward enough, with its increasingly disturbing mix of personal and business implications, without adding all sorts of interested local speculation about who Mark Channing might be romancing now.

"You told the woman who runs the general store that you were bringing me here?" Lindsay asked with evident dismay. "Why on earth would you do something like that?"

"Well, I didn't exactly give her your name, occupation and physical description. Just the general idea. Anything more, she assumed herself," he countered lightly, then taunted, "She'd have found out about you soon enough anyway. She's been trying to get me married off for several years now. I'm sure she'll be thrilled to meet you."

Despite her misgivings, a little flutter of excitement built in the pit of Lindsay's stomach at his casual reference to marriage. When she recovered from the unwanted, though definitely titillating reaction, she said tartly, "Not when she finds out my only interest in you is limited to discovering how distinctively you can sign your name on a contract.''

Mark regarded her doubtfully. ''That's your only interest?'' he queried softly, taking a step that brought him within mere inches of her. That little flutter returned in full measure and her heart palpitated erratically as he provocatively trailed a finger down her cheek and across her lips. Dark eyes, glittering with amusement, challenged hers.

Lindsay's breath caught in her throat. She didn't dare risk speaking, so she merely nodded. It was less emphatic than she might have liked.

''Like hell,'' he muttered disbelievingly, then walked off to put her suitcase in a room down the hall. She wished like crazy that her room was a minimum of four miles from his, but it looked like a very short hallway.

In the meantime she stood right where he'd left her, her feet planted so firmly in place she felt as if she'd been born and reared right there and might very well die there, if he touched her again like that and didn't do more. A whole lot more! A kiss would be a start, but only a start. She had a feeling that once she was in Mark Channing's arms, she'd never want him to let go.

That, Lindsay Tabor, she told herself sternly, is something you are not about to risk.

When he came back a moment later, he obviously noted that she hadn't budged and he smirked knowingly. ''Let's go skiing, bright eyes.''

He said it in that low, seductive voice that could have lured her into crime, sin and most certainly anything less dangerous. Skiing fell somewhere in the middle. In fact, by comparison, it was beginning to seem infinitely safer and more appealing by the minute.

As it turned out, however, her original assessment had been the accurate one. The skiing experience was pretty awful; if anything, even more dreadful than she had anticipated it might be. Its only virtue, as far as she could see, was that it did get her out of that house where all sorts of newly imagined dangers suddenly loomed.

In the meantime, though, her nose was cold. Her feet refused to do what she told them, not that she could blame them since they were standing on long, skinny strips of wood that skidded worse than bald tires. And her backside was frozen and sore from landing on it repeatedly.

They kept at the lesson for what seemed like an eternity, though in reality Lindsay knew that it was barely more than an hour. She kept telling herself she was scrappy, a born fighter, that she was not going to be defeated by a sport other people without her college education, law degree and responsible career could do as easily as walking. Even little bitty children could ski, she reminded herself in disgust as she toppled over again.

As a result of these internal pep talks, every time her skis shot out from under her, she got determinedly to her feet again and tried putting one foot cautiously in front of the other. As long as she simply picked them up and plunked them down, she did okay. But whenever she tried to glide in the smooth, easy motion that

Mark had patiently demonstrated over and over, she felt as though she were out of control and, arms whirling frantically and futilely, down she went. She thought about making snow angels while she was down there, but she wasn't feeling the least bit angelic. Besides, Mark pulled her back up almost immediately just so she could fall again. It confirmed her impression of his perversity.

"You'll do better tomorrow," he consoled, finally taking pity on her and helping her back into the house, where Shadow lifted his head and thumped his tail once in greeting, then went right back to his nap.

"If I live," she muttered, wishing she could go lie down in front of the fire and put her head on Shadow's back. She wondered if he'd mind or even notice. That dog seemed to need vitamins. On the other hand, he'd been inside in front of the fire, while she'd been outside freezing her tush off. It didn't take a genius to figure out which of them was in better shape physically and mentally.

"Once you've had a nice hot bath, you'll feel a whole lot better," Mark assured her. He regarded her hopefully. "You have to agree it was beautiful out there this afternoon. That sky was something. I've never seen it so blue. Have you ever seen anything quite so gorgeous?"

"The beach at Maui," she countered dryly, as she rubbed her icy hands together. They felt as though millions of tiny needles were jabbing them. She'd almost liked it better when they were numb.

"It's hardly the same."

"I'll say."

Mark looked crestfallen. "Didn't you like it at all? I thought maybe once you got the hang of it . . ."

"I haven't gotten the hang of it, remember? Not unless you're supposed to sit in the snow with your legs all tangled up with your skis."

"Tomorrow," he promised again and Lindsay felt a tiny little quiver of guilt. Here was a successful, handsome, rugged, virile man who seemed to want more than anything to please her, to share his special world with her, and she was behaving like an ungrateful wretch. Her mother would have a heart attack if she knew. She'd tell Lindsay that from now on she deserved whatever she met while flying in coach.

She tried to think of something positive to say just for her mother's sake, if nothing else. Words failed her.

"It really wasn't so bad," she offered finally. Even she recognized that it was a weak compliment at best, so she tried to put a little more enthusiasm into it. "It was . . . white out there. Very white. I like white a lot."

In fact, she thought to herself, she'd never seen so much white in her life outside of a medical thriller she'd watched being filmed in a hospital laundry last year. This white definitely had been better than that.

She sniffed, then sneezed. And sneezed again, harder. Her baleful glance at Mark was filled with blame.

"Good Lord, don't go catching a cold on me," he murmured, moving close enough to help her off with her snow-covered jacket. His gaze met hers and caught. "Then I'll never prove to you how wonderful this place is."

Lindsay didn't think he could ever prove that to her, if he provided a sauna and let her stay in it twenty-four hours a day. Still, there was something to be said for being in the same room with him. She felt as if she was getting warmer by the second. She also seemed to be having a great deal of difficulty breathing and she knew it was far too soon for pneumonia to have set in. It must have something to do with the fact that his very masculine hands were just beneath her chin, which seemed instinctively to want to nestle in their warmth. Before she could give in to that crazy urge, he was slowly unzipping her jacket in an oddly intimate, provocative gesture that warmed her right down to her toes. It was definitely better than brandy, more intoxicating and infinitely more exciting.

"I'll run your bath right away," he offered huskily, his hands lingering at her waist. It was an innocent enough offer, but Lindsay had a feeling that with very little encouragement he would be in that bath with her and, as appealing as it was, *that* would not be a good idea. Men and women who took baths together did not just get clean.

She took a deep breath, sneezed again and waved him away. "I can run my own bath."

A slow grin turned up the corners of his very inviting mouth. "Lordy, you're independent," he said with an exaggerated sigh, then relented, dropping his hands from her waist. "Okay, if it'll make you happy, you're on your own. I'll build the fire up a bit and start on dinner. You'll find towels and things in the bathroom cupboard. If you can't find something, just give a yell."

Among the "things" Lindsay found in the cupboard was a wide assortment of bubble bath. Pretending that she didn't give a darn why it was there, she selected one that was lilac scented and spilled it in the water that gushed from the faucet in a satisfyingly steamy stream.

Stripping off the damp layers of clothes that had only barely kept her from freezing to death, she stepped into the oversized tub and sank down in hot, soothing water and bubbles up to her chin.

"Ahh," she sighed gratefully. Now this was her idea of the perfect way to end the day. If only she had a glass of wine and a book, she'd be in heaven. She leaned back and shut her eyes. When she opened them, she glanced toward the ceiling and blinked. Unless she was losing her mind, there was a star twinkling up there. Had she frozen to death after all and gone to heaven? She tried closing, then opening her eyes again. More stars glittered back at her from a darkening sky. With a sort of dazed astonishment, she realized that Mark had a slanting skylight in his bathroom! And, as she had somehow known it would be, this tub was definitely big enough for two. The sensuality inherent in the architectural design of the room intrigued her and set off odd little tingling sensations, which crept slowly along her spine and settled low in her abdomen.

What a wonderful, romantic, sexy idea, she thought dreamily. She wondered if it had been his, then hated the possibility that it might not have been.

Lindsay Tabor! she thought in wonder. You are jealous! It was a first and she wasn't a bit pleased about it. She was actually envious of some unseen, unnamed and possibly nonexistent woman. She picked up a bar of soap and a washcloth and scrubbed until her skin turned bright pink, as if that might wash away the unwanted emotion. It didn't, though it got her very clean.

"Are you awake in there?" Mark's voice filtered through the door and, recalling his unceremonious entrance into her hotel room in the morning, Lindsay clutched the washcloth over rosy-tipped breasts that were still tingling from her overzealous washing.

"Of course, I'm awake."

"Just checking. Dinner will be ready in a few minutes."

"I'll be right there," she promised, pushing aside her jealousy along with the remaining bubbles and climbing out of the tub to envelop herself in a huge towel that had been hanging over a heated rack. It felt wonderful, but she didn't linger to enjoy the sensation. Quickly she dried herself and pulled on her preferred lacy bikini pants and bra. Immediately she felt more feminine and wondered fleetingly if that was such a hot idea. Mark already had her hormones operating in overdrive. She added the new jeans and thick, multicolored sweater in rust tones that flattered her coloring. Her short hair had curled into an auburn halo around her head and her cheeks were flushed. She decided to forego makeup, except for a bit of pale coral lipstick and a quick flick of mascara.

When she walked back into the living room, Mark's eyes brightened appreciatively and he walked toward her until they were standing toe-to-toe. That seemed to be his favorite position for carrying on a conversation. She wondered idly if he was nearsighted or if he was pointedly trying to be intimidating. If it was the latter, she'd have to tell him sometime that it was a very successful technique. He scared the daylights out of her with his sensuality, his romantic, poetic way with words and his outspoken admission of his attraction to her. Those fleeting, instinctive feelings that had stirred to life in the airport were crystallizing into very real, very tempting emotions with every additional minute she spent around him.

Her eyes focused square in the middle of his all-too-alluring chest. Hesitantly, she tilted her head until she was gazing up at his face. It disconcertingly appeared almost as flushed as she knew hers was.

"Feel better?" he inquired softly.

"Much," she said, the word barely squeaking out over vocal chords that seemed to be going into early retirement.

"You look terrific," he said huskily, as his head lowered to bring his lips dangerously close to her ear. "Umm. And you smell wonderful, too."

The whisper of breath that flickered along her neck heated her in a way that no blazing fire could have. His hands were resting on her waist again in a light caress that somehow seemed more binding than a tighter embrace would have been. She could take a single step back and be away from that touch and she knew it. Instead, she stayed right where she was, her heart thundering in anticipation, her gaze locked with his in a searching, penetrating duel that yielded no answers, only raised more questions. Dangerous questions.

"Dinner's going to get cold," he said at last, his voice a husky, reluctant whisper.

"Dinner?" she repeated blankly.

He grinned at her, breaking the tension of the moment, and teased, "You'll remember all about it after we start."

Once she'd sat down at a candlelit table to steak, baked potatoes, salad and a Beaujolais-Villages Nouveau wine, Lindsay realized that she was starved. But as the wonderfully simple meal filled her, something far more interesting happened. She began to forget all about the snow outside. She even began to forget why she was in Boulder in the first place. Slowly but surely, she fell even further under the spell of Mark Channing's considerable charms.

He was an admirable host, witty and intelligent and obviously drawn to her, though she still couldn't quite figure out why he had been so intent on this virtual kidnapping. She wasn't sure if it even mattered anymore. She was here now and, in the strangest way, she felt she belonged here. It was a sensation that puzzled and fascinated her. It probably should have terrified her, but she refused to examine it that closely. For the moment it was enough that she felt warm and mellow and desirable.

When they'd finished eating, she started to help clean up, but Mark waved her toward the sofa. "That can wait. Let's go sit by the fire."

They sank down side by side on the comfortable sofa with its dark-toned, overstuffed cushions. Shadow lifted his head slightly, noted their presence and moved a little closer, his head resting on Mark's boot.

"You know something, Lindsay Tabor?" Mark said softly, his fingers playing in the curls that edged her face, brushing all too casually against skin that seemed to burn with a fever of growing desire.

"What?" she asked breathlessly.

"You've never told me a thing about yourself. All last night you kept turning the conversation back to me. Now I want to know about you."

"There's not much to tell. Morrie gave you a pretty accurate summary."

Mark chuckled. "I don't think so. At least, that's not the Lindsay Tabor I've seen in the last twenty-four hours. Oh, you're stubborn and scrappy and bright all right, but you're funny and warm—"

"Now," she retorted dryly.

"I wasn't talking about the temperature." His fingers gently caressed the silky skin of her neck and the flames grew hotter deep inside her. "Why do you find it so difficult to admit you might be a caring, tender woman underneath that businesslike facade?"

"It's not a facade," she protested.

"Okay. Bad choice of words. But you're much more than a tough-minded lawyer. You're a woman," he said, his voice growing soft, weaving a magical spell. "A lovely, intriguing woman..." His lips hovered a mere hairsbreadth from hers. "A woman whom I want very, very much."

Firelight made his dark eyes sparkle with dazzling lights and Lindsay wanted nothing more than to lose herself in the desire she could read in those eyes. The coil of tension inside her was winding tighter and tighter until she thought she would explode with an unfamiliar longing. A tender touch, a persistent caress, a passionate kiss and she would be lost.

But those were emotions, demanding physical needs, drawing her to him. Intellectually, she knew it would be a dreadful mistake to give in to them. Not only did she have business to conduct with this man, she also had no intention of cluttering up her life with a serious involvement. And any involvement with Mark Channing would be serious, at least for her. He had reached some previously untouched part of her from the moment they'd met in the airport. His gentle, romantic words and warmly appreciative gazes had made her all too susceptible to possibilities and dreams she'd never before considered for her life.

It was odd how all that snow had managed to build a layer of ice around her heart again, only to have it melt beneath the blazing fire that danced beguilingly in Mark's eyes. The man clearly had more tricks up his sleeve and he seemed to have a psychologist's knack for unlocking long-buried thoughts.

Suddenly she was remembering those long-ago days when she'd had a complete family, a mother and a father who loved her and who filled the house with laughter and good times. Then she was remembering how awful it had been when it ended so abruptly. She never wanted to feel that kind of loss and anguish again.

"Hey, where'd you go?" Mark asked gently, wiping away a tear she hadn't even realized was rolling down her cheek.

Unable to speak through the unreleased sobs that choked her, she shook her head.

"I'm a good listener. Maybe it would do you good to talk about it," he suggested.

He waited, but for the longest time she still said nothing. "I can't," she finally said miserably. "Besides, it was a long time ago and it doesn't matter anymore."

"How can you say that, when it still makes you cry?"

She tilted her chin stubbornly. "Because I won't let it matter anymore."

He gathered her into his arms then and held her tightly, banishing the past and making her aware of only the present. Lindsay instantly felt incredibly safe and protected, as she hadn't felt in many years, until last night when Mark had performed the simple act of taking her hand in his and holding it until his strength had seemed to flow into her. How could a man she barely knew have such a reassuring impact on her? How could he know her needs so well? No one had ever seemed to suspect that she needed anything more than her own inner strength before. No one had ever sensed the vulnerability she fought so intensely to hide.

But although she was beginning to feel better, warm and cherished as though nothing could ever harm her again, Mark was still responding to her pain. There was so much compassion in his gaze. He seemed to understand her even though she hadn't revealed a thing.

"I wish it were that easy." he said simply.

"It has to be."

"No," he said tenderly, shaking his head and Lindsay realized he was speaking from his own experi-

ence. "It never is. Are you sure you don't want to talk
about it?"

"I wish I could," she said and meant it. She knew
intuitively that if anyone would empathize with her,
Mark would, but she didn't understand her feelings
clearly enough to express them.

"All it takes is getting the first words out," he said.
"They're always the hardest."

"No. First you have to figure out what it is you need
to say. I don't even know where to begin."

"This is a great place for thinking things through.
Maybe you'll figure it out while you're here."

He brushed a kiss across her forehead then and gave
her a comforting squeeze. "Go on to bed. You could
use a good night's sleep. We'll talk some more tomorrow."

She gazed into his eyes, expecting something more.
He smiled tenderly and repeated firmly, "Go on to
bed."

Lindsay walked to her room with conflicting emotions raging inside her. She was grateful that he had let
her go, that he had probed only so deeply and no further. But unwittingly he had brought to the surface
feelings and fears she hadn't experienced in years, and
she knew it was going to take more than a weekend in
this peaceful, serene environment to cope with them.

As if trying to deal with her long-buried memories
weren't bad enough, he had also stirred brand-new
emotions and desires. Used to keeping most members
of the opposite sex at arm's length, she was confused
and frightened by her longing to be more closely involved with this particular man. She was even more

puzzled by his failure to pursue the advantage he obviously knew he had. With very little effort they both knew he could have joined her in her bed tonight, and yet he had chosen to send her on alone, to leave her with her tumultuous thoughts.

Suddenly feeling a little lost, a little lonely, she gazed back at him. He was staring into the fire, and from the expression on his face she could tell that he had gone away into his private world, one that was far away from her and filled with a pain she couldn't begin to understand.

She wanted to go to him, to comfort him, as he had her, but she'd learned a few things about Mark Channing in the last twenty-four hours and she suspected that his pride was as strong as his sense of self-confidence. Whatever it was that had affected him so deeply, it was his burden alone. He would share it with her only when he was ready, just as she had her own fears and secrets to protect.

Six

Sunday morning Lindsay was awake practically at dawn, too emotionally wound up to sleep any longer. She'd tossed and turned all night trying to figure out why she was so reluctant to become even casually involved with a man as attractive, vital and intelligent as Mark Channing. For that matter, she wondered why for so many years now, she'd been running so hard to escape any type of involvement. There was no denying that she had been running. Too many men had tried to get close to her and failed.

She'd always told herself she wanted a meaningful career and that a relationship would only interfere with that goal. But she was established and successful now. She could afford to take time out for a personal life, and yet she had continued steadfastly to turn aside the overtures of most men. None of the others had been a particularly big loss, but she knew instinctively that Mark Channing was another story and perhaps that was the problem. He would never be easy to walk away from once she'd let him into her heart.

So why do I feel so strongly that I'd have to leave him behind? she wondered, and suddenly she was right back at the beginning of the same vicious circle. Maybe Mark was right. It could be about time she tried to find the words to explain her fears, first to herself and then perhaps to him. She resolved to try.

That decision made, she began to wonder again about the pensive state in which she'd left Mark last night. Had it been caused by something she'd said that reminded him of painful memories? She went over and over their conversation, trying to pinpoint anything that might have hit him too close to home. But the truth of the matter was she knew very little about Mark's personal life and only somewhat more about his professional life. Trent had packed her up and sent her on her way with the skimpiest briefing she'd ever had. It was one of the reasons she'd been so furious with her boss. She never liked to go into a situation without knowing everything necessary, and in this instance she knew next to nothing about David Morrow. Hell, she hadn't even known that he lived quietly in the mountains as Mark Channing.

Finally, tired of dealing with questions for which she had no answers, she threw off the warm covers and climbed out of bed. Hesitantly, recalling yesterday's disgustingly pale gray excuse for midmorning in Denver, she peeked through the blinds in her room and discovered shimmering streaks of gold in the sky. The sun here didn't even pretend to offer the warmth of California sunshine, but it had created a veritable fairyland of diamonds glittering on the snow.

She glanced at her watch and saw that it was barely seven a.m. By Mark's standards that was probably the middle of the day, but she didn't hear a sound anywhere in the rest of the house. He was either still asleep or already outside exploring the day's offerings. Ironically, she realized she wanted to be out there, too. Even the idea of actually mastering this ridiculous cross-country skiing seemed important in her muddled state of mind. Some of her brain waves must have frozen yesterday while she'd been out there rolling around in the snow.

She pulled on her ski outfit, which had miraculously dried overnight, and tiptoed down the hall, not wanting to wake Mark if he was still snug in his bed. In the living room she noted that the room was cold, the fire now no more than dying embers, and, to her surprise, Mark was sound asleep in front of it, still in his jeans and wool shirt, his dark hair tousled, his jaw shadowed with an early-morning beard.

Lindsay stared at him, an odd, yearning ache filling her. Even asleep, he was an impressive sight, though he looked uncomfortable with his tall frame scrunched up on the too-short sofa. She wondered again what turbulent thoughts had kept him awake so late that he had fallen asleep at last right where he was, rather than down the hall in his own room.

Lindsay got an afghan from her room and gently spread it over him, her hand lingering on his shoulder. She only barely resisted the urge to caress the dark stubble on his cheeks. Quickly, before she could give in to temptation, she pulled on her jacket and went out the door. As soon as she opened it to slip outside, Shadow rose up from his spot at Mark's side and followed her. His tail wagged hopefully.

"Okay, fellow, come on," she whispered as they went out into the icy morning air. A blast of bone-chilling wind hit her full force, but she pulled her bright turquoise knit cap farther down over her ears and kept going. She was determined not to be put off by the weather, no matter how awful it was. She was going to be gliding around on these damn skis like a pro by the time Mark woke up. Either that or she was going to break something important and spend the next month recuperating on some nice, warm beach at Trent Langston's expense.

With Shadow frolicking along beside her in a display of suddenly boundless energy that seemed to match her own high spirits, she clicked her boots into place on the skis and set off across the field behind the house. Every muscle in her body protested her renewed attempt to perform this unnatural act, but she persisted and suddenly she realized that she was actually gliding instead of stomping, her arms moving in tandem with her legs and all of her staying perpendicular to the ground.

"Shadow, I'm doing it," she called excitedly as the dog bounded back to her and barked. They were in the midst of a rowdy, joyous celebration, when Mark poked his head out the door, rubbing his eyes sleepily.

"What's all the noise about?" he mumbled, his morning voice husky.

Lindsay skied over to him, dropped her ski poles and threw her arms around his neck. "I did it. I actually skied."

Mark's arms instinctively wound around her and held her against his chest, his suddenly laughing eyes meeting hers. "It's not half bad once you catch on, is it?"

"It's wonderful," she said gleefully, then grinned at his smug expression. "Well, maybe not wonderful, but it's pretty great."

"I—"

"Don't say it," she warned. "If you even think about saying I told you so, I will take these skis off and wrap them around your neck."

He feigned fear. "I promise I won't say a word," he agreed quickly. "Besides, I much prefer having your arms around my neck anyway."

Lindsay suddenly realized the intimacy of their embrace and started to back away, but Mark shook his head. "Oh, no, you don't. You started this. You're not quitting on me now." He hesitated. "There is just one thing, though."

"What's that?"

"Do you suppose you could come back inside or wait until I get my jacket? I am about to freeze to death."

Lindsay started chuckling at the plaintive tone in his voice. "Interesting turn of events."

"Isn't it, though?" he agreed dryly. "So, what's it going to be?"

"You come out here. Shadow and I are having too much fun to come inside."

"Shadow?"

Lindsay looked around. The dog had vanished. She peered past Mark into the living room. He was flopped out in front of the fireplace again, apparently relieved that he no longer needed to chaperone her now that his master was awake to do it.

"Traitor," she muttered accusingly as Shadow's tail thumped once. She grinned at Mark. "Okay, you come out and play with me. I'll keep practicing."

The rest of the day held the same sort of magical spell that had begun in the morning. She and Mark skied for another hour, chatting amiably about everything from forest creatures and environmental protection to Sunday comics and freedom of the press. They carefully avoided discussing books and movies as if they both knew that to bring them up would lead to an inevitable fight about the contract that still sat untouched in Lindsay's briefcase.

When Mark said something that totally outraged her, something about women who worked getting too caught up in political office games to retain their natural femininity, Lindsay stopped, bent down and loosely packed a huge snowball in her mittened hands. Then she called out to him. When he turned around to see what she wanted, she threw it straight into his smug face.

"Why, you little..." he sputtered, advancing on her, as he brushed snow off his ruddy cheeks and out of his hair, where it glistened like multi-hued opals against black velvet.

Lindsay had the distinct impression from his menacing scowl that he was not coming after her to congratulate her on her aim. She began backing up. If she'd thought it difficult to learn to move forward on skis, she now discovered that it was virtually impossible to go backward, at least for her. Mark was on top of her before she could even consider simply turning around and skiing forward in the opposite direction.

"Come here, you little rebel," he ordered.

She stood her ground. "I am not a little rebel. I am a woman who can successfully combine a career and a personal life perfectly well, thank you very much," she said, conveniently dismissing the fact that her personal life consisted of an occasional movie with a friend and an endless number of salads eaten alone at night in front of a TV. "And except for this dumb underwear you've got me wearing, I am very feminine."

"Is that so?" he taunted, skiing closer. "Let me check that out."

"Take my word for it."

"Tsk, tsk," he retorted. "And you a lawyer."

"What does that have to do with anything?"

"You should know all about evidence. You can't build a good case without evidence."

She eyed him narrowly. "Exactly what evidence do you hope to gather?"

"I might be able to tell if you're as feminine as you say you are from a kiss," he suggested, as heat began to build slowly and persistently inside Lindsay until she felt as though she was again in front of the fire.

"My femininity is not at issue here."

"Oh, yes, it is. You brought it up, in fact."

"No. You brought it up."

"I merely made a general statement about the femininity of certain women in the business world. You took it personally. Now that you have, I think you ought to back up your statement."

"Sounds like a self-serving demand to me."

"Oh, I think a kiss might be worth both our whiles."

"And a kiss would do it?" she asked, suddenly breathless. "You're sure?"

He nodded. "It's a start."

"Well..."

Before she could complete the sentence, Mark's head had descended toward hers and his lips were teasing the corners of her mouth, his tongue flicking against her lips until they parted on a sigh. His arms went around her then and their mouths locked with a hungry urgency that robbed her of all strength. She felt weightless, as though he'd lifted her off the ground and carried her away to another time and place that was filled with warmth and sunshine and joy. She wanted that kiss to go on forever, but Mark's lips were leaving hers and then she really was in his arms, her legs dangling crazily with her skis clattering together like noisy wind chimes.

"Put me down, you idiot," she pleaded, laughing. "Where are you taking me?"

"Inside."

"Inside?"

"I think I need to gather more evidence."

"You can get all the evidence you need right here."

He looked her straight in the eye and shrugged, plunking her unceremoniously back on her feet, but not letting her out of his arms.

"If you say so," he said pleasantly. Too pleasantly, she realized too late. He began to unzip her jacket.

"Now what are you doing?" she asked, her eyes widening in dismay as she tried to bat away his all-too-persistent hands. She didn't seem to be doing a very effective job of it, either. Her jacket was unzipped and his hands were grazing breasts that were instantly taut and aching despite being underneath still more layers of clothes.

"I was wrong. There's more to this evidence stuff than just a kiss," he informed her airily.

"But you promised a kiss would do it," she responded, a hint of desperation in her voice. Two more minutes of this spiraling pleasure that curled through her and she wasn't going to be able to ask him to stop. If anything, she would be begging him to go on, to make love to her.

"One kiss. That's what you said," she repeated dazedly.

"That was before I knew that it was only the tip of the iceberg."

A little flicker of fighting spirit rallied. "You take a single layer of my clothing off out here and I will be an iceberg."

He grinned at her hopefully. "Then you're ready to come inside?"

She beamed back and nodded. "I am going inside," she said agreeably, then added, "but you're not. I think you need the Boulder equivalent of a cold shower. Go roll around in the snow.''

Mark's expression fell. "Now I know how Morrie must have felt," he said in a dejected tone. "You're cruel and heartless, just as I suspected. It's all that fighting for position in the business world."

"Don't think you're going to manipulate me into your bed, Mark Channing," Lindsay retorted, waving her ski pole at him threateningly. "I'll make love to you when I'm good and ready."

His eyes lit up and she had a feeling she'd just uttered a very backhanded commitment, one she'd had no intention of making.

"Then you will make love with me?" he said. "Soon?"

"When hell freezes over," she said defiantly, then looked around her at the icicles clinging to the tree branches and the never-ending snow that covered the ground like a thick winter blanket and wondered if it already had. Certainly the odds of her holding out much longer against Mark's increasingly provocative advances were not something they'd want to bet on in Las Vegas.

However, not once for the rest of the day, did he even brush up against her by accident, much less by design. They ate lunch, then spent the afternoon in front of the fire reading in companionable silence while classical music played softly on the stereo. Every now and then Lindsay would peer over the top of the book and watch Mark as he read, his brow furrowed in concentration. It was the first time she could ever recall being so at ease spending time with a man in an environment that didn't contain a desk or conference table. It was, in fact, the first time she'd had so much unplanned time stretched out in front of her to do with as she pleased. Right now simply being with Mark pleased her very much. She felt no need to entertain, no desire to be entertained. Just being with him gave her an enormous feeling of contentment.

Later, they fixed dinner together, battling over the proper way to do the lettuce for the salad. She thought it should be torn. He wanted to slice it into shreds. Stubbornly, they each fixed one their own way and traded the finished product.

"Okay, so it tastes the same," Lindsay grumbled, when they were sitting at the table. "I'm sure Craig Claiborne and Julia Child would be appalled if they saw lettuce all diced up into little shreds this way. Can you imagine this being served at the Four Seasons?"

"This isn't the Four Seasons," Mark retorted. "As for your experts, if they're that picky, I would never invite them to dinner. I refuse to have culinary snobs at my table."

"They would love this stew though. Did you make it?"

"Of course."

"What's in it?"

"Carrots, potatoes, onions, the usual."

Lindsay picked up a chunk of meat on the tip of her fork and held it in the air. "And this? It doesn't taste like beef."

"It's not. It's venison."

She lowered her fork slowly back to the bowl, her green eyes darkening in dismay. "As in Bambi?"

"Oh, dear heavens. You're not one of those."

"One of those what?"

"People who don't believe in hunting."

"How can you go out and kill an innocent little deer?"

"I don't kill innocent little deer. I kill grown-up deer and only for food, not just for the fun of it."

Lindsay shivered. "It's still cruel."

"You ate that steak last night without muttering a single whimper of protest."

"That was different."

"How? The cow didn't even have a fighting chance."

"I don't want to talk about it."

"Of course not, because you know you're not being logical."

"That's right. I'm being emotional and feminine. Not too long ago that's exactly what you wanted me to be."

"I think there's a difference."

Lindsay knew perfectly well there was, but she'd already lost this round and she had no desire to prolong his satisfaction at her defeat.

"Couldn't we talk about something else?" she asked as they moved into the living room and settled down at opposite ends of the sofa.

"Sure," he agreed with alacrity. "We can talk about you."

"I was thinking more about you. I really don't know very much about you except that you're a writer, that you live in the wilderness, have this insane attraction for snow and that you kill wild animals."

"I thought you didn't want to talk about that."

"Right. Let's stick to safer topics. You said you'd only lived here a few years. Where were you before that?"

"I traveled a lot. A writer can live almost anywhere and I did, mostly in Europe, though I spent one glorious summer in Bali and another one on a tiny island in the Caribbean. Every winter I went to Switzerland to a chalet in a small village in the Alps."

Lindsay hesitated, then finally asked what she'd really wanted to know all along. "Alone?"

"Sometimes," he said briefly, his tone clearly slamming the door shut on the subject.

"Mark, can I ask you something?"

He studied her cautiously, then nodded. "Sure."

"Have you ever been in love?"

"I'm thirty-nine. What do you think?" he replied cryptically.

"I think you're avoiding the question."

He tried one of his dazzling smiles on her. "Who was it who said that the only thing that matters is the present?"

"Probably some man who didn't want to talk about the past."

"Smart man."

"Not really. The past is largely responsible for the present."

"Then let's talk about yours some more," he said, turning the conversation right back around on her. She considered it one of his less attractive habits.

"What are you so afraid of?" he asked.

"Who said I'm afraid?"

"It's in your eyes every time we start to get too close."

"That's just your imagination."

"Is it?" he asked skeptically, then challenged, "In that case, come over here by me."

Lindsay hesitated just a second or two too long. By the time she met Mark's gaze again, his eyes were twinkling. "I rest my case."

"Just because I don't want to have a meaningless little fling with you doesn't mean I'm afraid."

"It wouldn't be meaningless between us and you know it."

Lindsay sighed. "Okay," she said at last. "Maybe you're right and maybe that is the problem. I don't want any involvements in my life."

"Why? I got the feeling last night that something had happened to make you lock yourself away from the world."

"I'm not exactly locked away from the world. I'm traveling all over it."

"Alone."

"Yes."

"Why? You're a beautiful woman, easy to be with, intelligent. Why would you choose to be alone? And don't try to dance around that, because I know it has to be by choice. For the last two days I've watched you systematically shut me out and I don't think I'm the first man you've done that to. You're too good at it."

"I learned very early that you can't count on other people, even the ones you love the most," she said matter-of-factly, though there was a growing ache in her heart.

He reached out and captured her hand in his, his gaze warm and tender. "Who hurt you? Who hurt you so badly that you don't trust anyone?"

Lindsay could feel the tears welling up in her eyes as she remembered in precise and horrifying detail the day they'd come to tell her mother that her father was dead, that the plane he'd been on had crashed into the side of a mountain and there were no survivors. She'd blamed him for leaving them. God, how she'd hated him for that, even though she'd known she was wrong.

"It wasn't his fault," she said shakily now. "He didn't mean to leave us alone. I know he didn't mean to do it."

"Who?"

"My father."

"He walked out on you?"

"No. It was nothing like that. He was killed in a plane crash. He traveled a lot and one time the plane just didn't make it back. I was nine years old, and all of a sudden one of the people I loved the most was gone and it didn't make any sense. It hurt so much."

"Oh, I'm so sorry," Mark said, drawing her into his arms and holding her against his chest. Once more, she could feel his strength seeping into her, easing the pain. "That explains everything. You've spent your whole life trying to avoid another loss like that, haven't you?"

Suddenly it was clear to her. That was exactly what she'd been doing. She'd known it subconsciously, but she'd never before allowed the thoughts to surface so that she could deal with them, just as she'd forced herself to board plane after plane, each time terrified that she would die as her father had.

"I suppose so," she admitted, knowing that it was more than mere supposition. It was fact.

"I know exactly how you feel, but you can't live your life in a glass cage to protect yourself against hurt."

"I don't see why not. I'm busy. I have friends. I love my job."

"And you spend your nights all alone."

"I don't need anyone to share my nights," she said stubbornly.

"I felt that way once, too, but then I realized I wasn't living. I was only existing. Don't let that happen to you, bright eyes. It would be such a waste."

The intensity of the warning and the warmth and concern behind it left Lindsay shaken and emotionally drained. Reaching deep inside herself to admit the truth about her fears had taken a devastating toll, more than she could handle in one night.

"I think I'd better get to bed," she said, wondering if Mark would try to stop her. But, once again, he let her go with only a brief, tantalizing kiss.

"Night, love."

By the time Lindsay finally climbed into her bed, every one of her senses seemed to be screaming in frustration. She was alone again, and, as adamant as she'd been about not needing anyone, for the first time in her life she didn't want to be alone. She wanted to be back in Mark's arms as she had been earlier. It was a pull more powerful than anything she had ever felt before and she knew that sooner or later she was going to have to do something about it. Running away seemed like a very good idea.

By the time Monday morning rolled around after another virtually sleepless night, she wanted more than ever to go back to Los Angeles. She had admitted during the night that she was becoming entangled in something with Mark that she was afraid to face: her own sensuality, her own rapidly building physical desires, desires that would lock her into the very kind of relationship she'd always been so careful to avoid.

But leaving Mark Channing to put her life back on an even keel was not just a simple case of packing her bag and going to the airport. There was still the matter of the contract to be settled, and try as she might, Mark seemed to be oblivious to every subtle attempt she made to get him to read it, much less discuss it. Even her more direct suggestions were met with evasive responses and tactical retreats that would have made any army commander proud. They only infuriated her.

"Mark," she finally began as they sat sipping coffee after lunch on Monday afternoon. They had spent the morning laughing like a couple of carefree kids as they built a huge lopsided snowman with a crooked button smile, a carrot nose and an old hunting cap sitting jauntily on his head. It had been fun, but the time for fun was over. She was becoming far too ensnared in a way of life that was all wrong for her.

"You promised me you'd read this contract, if I spent the weekend with you. The weekend's up and I have to go back," she said, rather proud of her decisive, no-nonsense tone. "Trent will be expecting me."

"Call him," Mark suggested blandly.

Lindsay glowered at him. So much for her power play. She knew exactly what calling Trent would accomplish: nothing. Her boss would let her stay here until the flowers bloomed in July if it meant that she'd come back with a deal to have Mark write a screenplay based on his latest book. It was Trent's current obsession, and no cost was too high when Trent Langston was personally obsessed with a project. He wouldn't help her. She was going to have to get out of this emotional minefield on her own.

"Mark, please. I really need to go back. I have other things to take care of."

He regarded her curiously. "Personal things? Is there another man in your life after all?"

The way Mark phrased the question and the darkly dangerous look in his eyes implied that he was in her life now and had every intention of staying there without sharing her with anyone else. That look posed a definite threat to any possible lingering commitments from her past. Fortunately, she supposed, there were none to worry about.

"No," she admitted at last. "You know perfectly well after last night that there's no man. I just have other work to do. It's been piling up while I chased you around the country."

"Now that you've found me are you really having such a miserable time?"

Lindsay bit her lip and refused to meet his penetrating gaze. That was precisely the trouble. She wasn't having a miserable time at all. She was enjoying being with Mark all too much. She was beginning to count on their long talks, on his gentle teasing, the increasingly more demanding touches that had suddenly abated, leaving her yearning for their resumption. She was beginning to want him in her life and that terrified her. Even though she was starting to understand why she'd always kept men at arm's length, it didn't mean she could change it overnight.

"I'm not here to have a good time. I'm here to get you to read the damned contract and sign it."

"You work too hard."

"How would you know?"

"I can tell. If you could have seen yourself Friday night..." He shook his head disapprovingly. "You looked like an exhausted, woebegone little waif."

"If I looked that lousy, I'm surprised you were so hot to take me in."

"That's exactly why I was so determined to take you in. I wanted to see some sparkle in those beautiful green eyes of yours."

Lindsay gave him her most beguiling smile. "You should just see the sparkle when I get a signed contract in my hands."

"I never promised I'd sign it," he reminded her. "Only that I'd read it."

"When?"

"When the time is right."

"Damn it, Mark! When will that be? I can't stay here forever," she said desperately. "I have other work to do."

"If you ask me, you're running away."

"From what?"

His gaze caught hers and she could see the knowledge that lit those black eyes until they burned with an exciting flame of passion.

"Only you can answer that one. Think about it," he suggested, as he calmly pulled on a jacket and went outside for a walk, Shadow bounding along beside him.

While he was gone, Lindsay did think, though not about Mark's taunting question. She already knew the answer to that: she was running from him. What puzzled her more was his ability to turn any conversation away from himself and back to her. While she had revealed so much last night, allowed herself to become increasingly vulnerable, he had remained a charming enigma. No amount of sensitive probing had revealed the reason for his brooding silences, the distant stares. It bothered her that even as she was growing to trust him, perhaps even to fall a little in love, if she were to admit the whole truth, he didn't seem to trust her at all. If for no reason other than that, it was time to retreat to the safety of her own environment, where she could regroup her defenses.

Even more than wanting to escape from an emotional situation she wasn't prepared to handle, though, she'd come to realize that these last few days had been a fantasy in other ways as well. She'd hardly noticed being virtually stranded in the middle of nowhere because Mark was constantly showering attention on her...talking to her, skiing with her, playing backgammon, simply sitting by her side while they were both engrossed in their own reading or thoughts.

But that closeness and attentiveness wouldn't last forever. It couldn't be sustained day in and day out over a lifetime, even if two people were madly in love. For one thing, sooner or later Mark would have to go back to writing, shutting her out for hours on end. What would she do then? She'd never be able to bear the loneliness. Perhaps one of the greatest paradoxes in her life was that while she was pushing people away to avoid commitment and loss, she was at the same time terrified of being alone.

Seven

Lindsay didn't have to wait long to find out what living in the middle of nowhere with Mark would really be like on any kind of permanent basis. Not that he'd exactly asked her to stay forever, she reminded herself. He had, however, given her plenty of indications over the last few days that he wasn't in any hurry for her to leave.

Still, when she woke up early Tuesday morning and found that he was already locked away in the den, it depressed her. She could hear his typewriter rapidly clacking along in a steady, intense way that did not invite interruptions and she immediately felt as shut out of his life as if there'd been a Do Not Disturb sign hanging on the closed door.

Trapped by Trent's obsession with this movie project, ensnared by her growing physical and emotional response to Mark and left at loose ends with only the sound of the typewriter to interrupt the endless silence, she began to feel cut off from the world for the first time since she'd arrived in Colorado. She had a feeling that if she screamed her head off, the only one for miles who'd notice or care would be Shadow, who'd been sneaking into her room since the very first night and sleeping at the foot of her bed.

Lindsay wasn't particularly surprised by the stark sensation of loneliness, only that it had taken so long to overcome her. Obviously Mark's attentiveness had kept it at bay. Now that he was hard at work again there was nothing to occupy her usually active mind.

No newspapers were delivered to the door way out here. They apparently collected for days at the general store until Mark went to pick them up. During the idle time they'd spent just sitting together in front of the fire, she'd read every back issue of the *Rocky Mountain News* and *Denver Post*, all of his magazines, plus those she'd bought at the Los Angeles airport. She'd even gone through every bit of work she'd thrown into her briefcase before leaving the office.

Bored, increasingly resentful of Mark's sudden defection, and resigned to the idea that she had accomplished nothing regarding the contract and wasn't likely to, she called Trent, hoping for a reprieve. His greeting dashed her hopes and made her mood even more foul than it already was.

"Where the hell have you been?" he snapped with more than customary rudeness, when he finally took the call after leaving her on hold for a solid fifteen minutes.

"Where the hell do you think I've been?" she snapped right back. "You sent me on a fool's errand and I've been following your orders."

"You're not in Denver," he accused. "I called that blasted hotel yesterday when you didn't show up for work or call in. They said you checked out first thing Saturday morning."

"That's not exactly true."

"Lindsay, don't play games with me. I'm in no mood for them. Either you're there or you're not there."

"I am not at the hotel. Your Academy Award winning writer checked me out."

"Then where the hell are you now?"

"At his place."

"Ahhh. I see," he said, his voice smoothing out with distinct pleasure. Trent was thoroughly disgusting when he thought one of his plans was working out just the way he'd intended. He took a certain amount of perverse delight in manipulating people like pawns in a high-powered chess game.

"You don't see a damn thing, you bloody idiot. I'm stranded out here in the damned wilderness with nothing to do, while your writer friend is holed up in the den pounding away on his typewriter."

"Is he writing the screenplay?" he asked hopefully.

"For all I know he's writing a letter to his mother."

"Has he signed the contract?"

Her voice was thick with sarcasm, she retorted, "Would I still be here if he had?"

"Only you can answer that, my little dove," he replied with exaggerated suggestiveness. He wouldn't have used that tone if Lindsay'd been in the same room. She'd thrown his prized crystal paperweight at him for far less.

She and Trent Langston were a more than even match most of the time. That was why he'd hired her. Even though he loved to shove his employees around, he only respected those who shoved right back. Lindsay not only shoved, she kicked and screamed. Usually.

Now she only pleaded plaintively, "Trent, I want to come home."

"Fine," he agreed cheerfully. "As soon as he signs, you can hop the next flight."

"You don't understand. I want to come back now!"

"Then get him to sign the contract now."

"Have you ever met Mark Channing?"

A bewildered silence greeted her question. Then he demanded irritably, "Who the hell's Mark Channing?"

"David *Mark Channing* Morrow."

"Oh. Yeah. I met him once. At one of those awards ceremonies or something. We didn't talk business or anything, but he seemed like a nice enough guy. Why?"

"A nice enough guy," she mimicked derisively. "The man is about as stubborn as an old mule that's made up its mind to stay in the barn. He's an awful lot like you, come to think of it."

"Lindsay!"

"Well, he is. He won't look at the contract, much less talk about it. I even stuck it in the middle of a magazine he was reading, but he threw it back on the table like it was just a dumb bookmark and went right back to an article about some actor's crusade to save the wilderness. Maybe if you offered to buy him his own mountain, he'd listen to reason," she suggested dryly.

"If you know of one and it's not too expensive, try it."

"Trent, I was kidding," she muttered in exasperation.

"I'm not."

Lindsay sighed. "No. I know you're not. If I happen to pass a mountain with a For Sale sign on the peak, I'll check it out."

"Good. You hang in there, Lindsay. I know you can pull this off."

"Exactly how long am I supposed to hang in here?"

"Until he signs."

"Then send some information on my retirement benefits," she suggested bitterly. "I may be a very old lady by then."

"Knowing how you feel about cold weather, I doubt you'll let him put you off that long. Bye, kiddo. Got to run."

"Trent!"

It was too late. He'd already hung up and she knew perfectly well there was no pressing call or important meeting awaiting him. He didn't want to give her any more time to try to wheedle him into letting her leave.

Not that he was likely to take pity on her anyway. Men like Trent did not make their fortunes by being kind and thoughtful where their employees were concerned. They made them by being single-minded. Trent did that better than anyone she'd ever known.

Resigned to her fate, she went into the kitchen and fixed herself some toast and tea and took it into the living room. She scanned Mark's haphazardly arranged bookshelves, marveling at the diversity of his taste in literature. Finally she found a thick novel she'd been wanting to read since its release two years earlier and settled down in front of the fire with Shadow sprawled out on the floor right next to her.

She should have been thoroughly relaxed, grateful to have some time to spend to herself after months of nonstop traveling and high-pressure assignments, but instead she continued to feel incredibly edgy. The fact of the matter was that she had no experience at relaxation. She usually avoided it like the plague, filling her time with business meetings, research and strategy sessions until she was so exhausted that she fell immediately to sleep the minute her head hit whatever pillow in whatever city she happened to be in.

As if this unwanted vacation weren't frustrating enough, the book she'd waited so long to read bored her to tears. It was one of those trashy, mindless concoctions of sex, violence and power struggles that would probably make millions as a television miniseries.

"I can't stand it," she finally muttered, snapping the book shut.

She sat on the floor and did a series of exercises, though muscles she'd never known existed until she'd taken up skiing screamed in protest with each leg lift and sit-up. Shadow cocked his head, watching her activity and listening to her muttered curses, then settled right back down.

When she couldn't do another single stretching exercise, she found a deck of cards and tried playing solitaire. She lost.

Finally, in desperation, she went back to her room and bundled up in her horrible winter underwear, slacks, jacket and boots, pulled on her cap and mittens and went outside, amazed that she actually felt better with the fresh air whipping around her. It cleared her head of all sorts of confusing thoughts about Mark, murderous thoughts about Trent and her own range of insecurities that had been surfacing more and more frequently over the past few days. They were insecurities that she'd deluded herself had been long overcome. Instead, she was discovering that they'd merely been buried, awaiting a situation like the one she was experiencing with Mark to surface again.

When she reached the end of Mark's driveway, her boots crunching on the ice-covered snow, she turned down the road in the direction of the general store. Maybe there she'd find some lively company to offer further distraction from her disturbing thoughts. At the very least she could pick up any newspapers and magazines that had come in for Mark, so she could occupy herself for the rest of the day.

She came upon the little shop about twenty minutes later, its front porch piled high with stacks of wood, a welcoming puff of smoke curling from the chimney. She stomped her feet to get the snow off her boots, then went inside. An old man with a healthy, graying beard and a pipe was sitting in front of an old wood-burning stove and a woman she knew immediately must be Mrs. Tynan was working behind the counter, piling groceries into a bag for a couple who seemed to be tourists. They were asking for directions to a lodge Lindsay knew was farther up the side of the mountain.

"You look half-frozen," the old man said to her, gesturing to a chair close to the stove. "Sit down here and rest a spell, young lady. This old stove ain't much to look at, but it'll warm you right up."

"Thanks."

"So," he said, dragging the word out as he scrutinized her closely. "You must be Mark Channing's gal. Heard tell he had a pretty young visitor up at his place."

Lindsay winced. It was just as she'd expected. The grapevine was in fine working order. Not that it had had far to travel from Mrs. Tynan to the man sitting beside her stove. It still made her uncomfortable to be thought of as *Mark Channing's gal*, when she wasn't quite sure Mark Channing was thinking of her at all.

"I'm visiting Mr. Channing on business for a few days," she said stiffly.

"Hmmph," the old man said with a toothy smile. "So that's what you young folks call it. Ain't nothing the matter with two people living together as far as I can tell. Nobody around here gives a hang anyway, leastways that's what I've been telling Grace for the last ten years."

He cast a sly, but adoring glance at the trim, wiry woman behind the counter, who was pointedly ignoring him. He shrugged. "Guess the old prune likes living by herself."

She reeled around at that and gave him a drop-dead glare from frosty blue eyes.

"It's better than living with you, Jeb Davis. It's bad enough that you stink up the store with that pipe of yours. I'll not have you stinking up my house," the woman retorted, though there was genuine affection in her voice.

"Hmmph. It's your loss," he grunted. "No point in these young ones making the same mistake."

"Jeb, you old coot, mind your own business," the woman said as she came out from behind the counter and held out her hand to Lindsay. "I'm Grace Tynan. Don't mind Jeb. His mouth always did operate faster than his brain."

"Lindsay Tabor," she said as she gazed up into a kindly, weathered face, from which those brilliant, cornflower-blue eyes now sparkled back at her. She could see the snap and vinegar that Mark had alluded to in this woman, but she also sensed the wry sense of humor and, more important, the comforting gentleness that would materialize the instant a person was in need of it. For some reason, she wanted this woman to like her, perhaps because she knew instinctively it would be important to Mark.

"I really am here on business," she repeated in what she hoped was a convincing tone.

"Too bad," Grace Tynan said in a low, gravelly voice that was filled with disappointment. Lindsay knew that she was about to ignore her own advice to Jeb. "I've been hoping Mark would meet someone who'd look after him and you're the first woman I ever recall him bringing up here. Thought maybe you'd be the one. If any man needs a wife to soften him up, he does."

Soften him up? Lindsay looked at Mrs. Tynan peculiarly. Mark wasn't hard. A bit of a loner maybe, but he was kind and gentle and fiercely protective. Not that she was about to share her impressions with this pair. They seemed to be hoping for a wedding announcement, and since she couldn't give them that, she figured she'd better just hold her tongue.

"What business do you have with Mark, little lady?" Jeb asked bluntly. "You from one of those publishers back East?" The way he said it, the East Coast sounded no better than an overcrowded den of iniquity.

"No. I work for a movie studio. We want him to do the screenplay from one of his books."

"Don't set much store in movies myself," Jeb said. "I like watching real people. They're a whole lot more interesting."

"Why don't you just say it, Jeb? You love to sit around and spy on other folks' lives and then gossip about it."

"That's not so, Grace Tynan. I'm no more a gossip than you are. You were at your best when half the electric and phone lines around here went down in that blizzard last winter and everyone depended on you for the latest news.''

"Oh, hush up, Jeb," she retorted as Lindsay grinned at the two of them. It sounded to her like they might as well be married, the way they bickered affectionately. She had a feeling Grace Tynan and Jeb Davis would have one heckuva passionate romance, if they ever gave it half a shot.

Grace glared at Jeb, then turned to Lindsay. "Which book do you want Mark to do?" she asked. "I've read 'em all."

"*Velvet Nights.*"

Grace Tynan's face immediately fell and her warm smile vanished. "*Velvet Nights*? Oh, honey, I wouldn't push him on that, if I were you."

"Why not?" Lindsay asked, puzzled by the oddly intense warning.

"Well, you'd best be asking him that, but I've always had the feeling that there was something right disturbing to him about that book."

"What makes you think that?"

"Oh, it was nothing he came out and said, you understand. It's just that usually he'd go down to the local library after one of his books came out and hold a discussion group. Folks around here are mighty proud of him and it was always a big deal," she explained and it was obvious that she shared the community's pride. Again, Lindsay sensed that a special bond existed between this woman and Mark, a bond that might help her to understand him, if only Grace Tynan would open up to her and share her insights.

"Did something different happen when *Velvet Nights* came out?" she asked.

"Sure did. The minute that book hit the stores, he just holed up in that cabin of his, same as he did when he first bought the place. Wouldn't see a soul. I'd take his groceries and mail to him and he'd thank me, real polite as always, but he never let me past the front door. Before that we'd always sit and have a cup of tea and a good chat. He'd tell me stories about the places he'd been and the people he'd met. I'd tell him what was going on around here. But not after *Velvet Nights*. Seemed like that book took something out of him. He was hurtin' real bad, honey. I'd hate to see all that stirred up for him again."

At last Lindsay was beginning to understand that Mark's avoidance of her, once he knew that Trent Studios wanted him to write that particular screenplay was part of a pattern. She still didn't understand why. Why had he even written a book that disturbed him so?

"How long did he shut himself away like that?" she asked, trying to imagine him lost and lonely in that cabin with only Shadow for company. The image tugged at her heart and she wished she'd known him then, that she'd been here for him. That stirring of protectiveness was as much of a surprise to her as the comfort she'd taken in Mark's tenderness toward her. She was so lost in her own thoughts that she almost missed what Grace Tynan was saying.

"It took about three months for him to come around," she recalled. "One day he just turned up here cheerful as could be, picked up his mail, bought a few supplies and chatted like he'd been here all along. He's seemed right as rain ever since, leastways until a couple of weeks ago, when he got a letter from that agent of his. His face clouded over and he took off out of here like a bat out of hell. I thought for sure the snow'd melt right out of his path, he was so hot under the collar.''

That must have been the letter from Morrie telling him about the offer from Trent Studios, the letter that started her game of hide and seek with him, Lindsay realized.

"I think I'd better be getting back," she said suddenly. It was time she and Mark had this out once and for all. She needed to understand his reluctance to do *Velvet Nights*. She was convinced now that there was far more to it than simple stubbornness or, as Trent had been convinced, greediness for a better contract. If she knew why he was so adamant, perhaps she could convince Trent to back off as well.

"Looks like we're about to get some more snow. You sure you wouldn't like a cup of tea to warm you a bit before you go?" Mrs. Tynan asked. "I've got the pot all ready."

"No, thanks. Another time."

"Then you'll be here awhile?"

"I'm not sure."

"Well, you come back anytime, honey. You're always welcome. Maybe you and Mark'd like to come for dinner one night?"

"I'll tell him you asked," Lindsay promised, though she had a few things to settle with Mr. Mark Channing before they went gallivanting around the countryside like some blissfully happy couple.

On the walk back, as snow began to swirl around her, first in a teasing flurry and then in a steady, thick wall of white, Lindsay turned over in her mind everything Mrs. Tynan had said and tried to make sense of it. Unfortunately, she hadn't had the chance to read *Velvet Nights* before Trent had sent her off on her whirlwind chase, so she had none of the insights the book itself might have given her. Oddly enough, now that she thought about it, there hadn't been a single copy on Mark's bookshelves, though his other books had been there.

Well, they'd just have to talk about the book and what it meant to him. If the man could write, he shouldn't be lacking in verbal skills. He should be able to explain his attitude about this and make her understand once and for all.

After a few more minutes, she was no longer able to think about what she and Mark needed to discuss. She had to concentrate on finding her way. The road was covered with new snow and the landmarks she'd noted on the way to the store were difficult to spot through the cloud of thick, wet flakes that pelted her. Though she'd never been caught in a snowstorm before, she wasn't particularly concerned, just cold. She was certain she was heading in the right direction and knew that soon she was bound to spot the old stone post that marked the driveway up to Mark's house.

Long before she saw the entrance, though, she heard Mark calling her name. She shouted back and

Shadow bounded up to her, putting his paws on her chest and licking her face.

"Shadow!" she protested, just as Mark seemed to materialize beside her.

"Hi," she said brightly, not noticing that he was in an absolute state of panic, his dark eyes shadowed with a barely concealed terror.

"Where the hell have you been?" he said, grasping her arms so hard, she could feel his fingers biting into her flesh even through the thick layers of clothing. Suddenly she saw the panic in his eyes and realized he was restraining himself from shaking her only with great effort. For a moment, she was almost frightened.

"Let go," she demanded. "You're hurting me. What on earth is wrong with you?"

Instantly, his hands dropped guiltily to his sides and he took a deep breath. This time when she gazed closely at him, the panicky expression she had seen before had been replaced by relief. The intensity of those responses startled her. He really had been terrified.

"You're okay then?" he asked insistently.

"Of course, I'm okay. Why wouldn't I be?"

"How long have you been out here?"

"Not that long. You were so busy writing, I decided to go for a walk."

"In a damned blizzard?"

"It wasn't snowing when I left."

"You could have gotten lost."

"I knew where I was. I only went down to the general store. I've been talking to Mrs. Tynan and Jeb.

They're quite a pair, by the way. She wants us to come to dinner.''

"That's nice," he muttered distractedly, then gazed into her eyes with a look that reflected his earlier urgency. "Lindsay, please, don't ever leave the house again without telling me."

At first she felt guilty for apparently having scared him by going for a walk on her own without even so much as leaving a note. Then, as she thought about the way he had abandoned her this morning, left her to her own devices, then hit her with this absurdly patronizing lecture, she grew increasingly infuriated.

"I'm a grown woman. I can take care of myself."

"You don't know anything about a place like this. You don't realize what could happen, how easily you could get lost. Please. Stay inside unless I'm with you."

"I will not! I'll go anywhere anytime I damn well please," she retorted. "If I'm stuck out here and you're going to shut yourself away and work, then I have to have something to do. I can't just sit around and twiddle my thumbs. I'm used to being busy."

All of her fury and pent-up frustration suddenly erupted in a no-holds-barred screaming match—at least on her part. Mark, all of his earlier anger gone now, just listened as she ventilated her fury. Now he was coolly rational, which further irritated her.

"Lindsay, I'm sorry I left you alone this morning. When I get an inspiration about something, I have to get it down on paper before I lose it. I didn't even realize you'd gotten up until I came looking for you and saw you were gone. Then when the snowstorm started,

I guess I panicked a little," he admitted sheepishly. "I wasn't trying to dictate your actions."

"It sure as hell sounded like you were," she said, not the least bit placated by the apology. The man's arrogance was appalling.

"You just don't know your way around here. Something could happen and I wouldn't have even known you'd gone out."

Suddenly it was all too much for her—the emotional intensity, the isolation, Mark's temporary abandonment and his insistent refusal to even look at the contract.

"I hate it here," she snapped at last, not caring that her words seemed to cut straight through to his heart. She could see the pain reflected in his eyes, which had turned dark and stormy, like a turbulent night sea.

"I want to go home," she added stubbornly anyway. It was beginning to seem more and more urgent that she get away.

He stared into her eyes for one long, heart-wrenching second, then sighed heavily. "I'm not stopping you."

"Yes, you are. You know very well I can't go back to Los Angeles until you've at least read the damned contract. Trent and I had that one out on the phone this morning and he made his position very clear."

"So you did call him?"

"Yes."

"What did he say?"

"To stay here until you come around."

"And that's the only reason you're staying?"

Despite the oddly hurt look in his eyes, she nodded.

"Okay," he said at last. "Let's go inside. I'll read the damned contract."

She was astounded by his sudden reversal and, perversely, wounded. Maybe he was ready for her to go, too. Perhaps that was why he'd shut himself away this morning, to give her a message that he no longer wanted her around, that the initial attraction had worn off once she'd let him know that she wouldn't be hopping into bed with him. Considering his reaction a moment ago to her absence, his seeming vulnerability and his very obvious fear for her safety, the explanation didn't make much sense, but the possibility hurt more than she wanted to admit.

"You'll really read it and give it some thought, so I can get back to Los Angeles?" she said more quietly.

"If that's what you want."

"It's what I want." Ironically she felt no particular satisfaction in the victory. She got the contract out of her briefcase, where she'd put it after her several attempts to leave it under his nose had failed, and handed it to him. Then, suddenly cold deep inside, she poured herself some brandy and waited.

While he read it, she watched him intently, chewing on her nails. When she noticed what she was doing, she wanted to throw her brandy snifter at him. She hadn't bitten her nails since junior high. At least back then, it had been over something simple like a math test and she'd been able to stop it once she'd passed.

But there was nothing simple about Mark Channing. If she'd ever thought there might be, her conversation with Mrs. Tynan had dispelled that idea once and for all. And even if she left Boulder tonight, she had a feeling she would not be leaving Mark behind. It was far too late for that. No matter where she went now or how long she was gone, she would carry his image and the memory of his tender, erotic touches in her heart.

Eight

Okay," Mark said flatly a half hour later, his voice empty of emotion. His tone sent a chill down Lindsay's spine. "I've read every clause, every one of Trent Langston's crazy, outrageous attempts at bribery. Now what?"

"It's not bribery." She paused, as his dark brows arched skeptically, and wondered exactly how straightforward she should be. Usually it was best not to give too much away. Never let the seller know how badly you want what he's offering, but in this case Mark wasn't offering anything. She might as well just go for it, lay all of her cards on the table. She gave Mark one of her most convincing, executive sales presentation smiles. His expression didn't change. He still looked very, very doubtful.

"Well, it's not exactly bribery," she amended. "Trent fell in love with *Velvet Nights* the minute he read it. He very badly wants to see this movie made. He admires your film work and he wants you to be the one to do it. I shouldn't tell you this, but you already suspect it anyway: he'll offer you whatever you want. Just name it."

"How about the moon? I think it's the only thing he's left out."

"Don't be ridiculous. Surely you see how advantageous this deal would be to you," Lindsay said persuasively, though she was more convinced than ever that she was fighting a losing battle. His jaw was set and there was no sign of those devastating dimples she'd grown to love. Whatever his reasons, Mark had made his decision a lifetime ago and he'd read the contract now only to humor her.

"How? I already have enough money for the lifestyle I like. You know how much I love it here. I have no desire to spend three or four months in L.A. or on location. Without trying to sound immodest, I already have an established reputation as a screenwriter. What exactly is this deal giving me that I want or need?"

Lindsay didn't have an answer for him, though she tried every argument she could think of, including Trent's only partially facetious offer to buy him a mountain all his own. Mark didn't even smile and the end result was the same: he remained stubbornly adamant; he was determined not to do the movie for Trent Studios.

"I won't do the movie for anyone else, if that's what you're thinking."

"But why?"

"*Velvet Nights* is very personal to me," he said tersely, all of the laughter gone from his dark-as-onyx eyes as he confirmed what Grace Tynan had intuitively suspected. His lips were set in a tight, angry, forbidding line. He wore a fierce expression that almost anyone else would have quickly decided to respect.

But Lindsay carefully ignored the ominous look on his face and tried to remember that she was here to do a job, not to worry about Mark Channing's personal hang-ups or her own growing reluctance to back him into a corner. She had to admit it was getting increasingly difficult to do. If it had been up to her, she would have thrown in the towel long ago and told him to forget the whole thing if it was going to make him this unhappy. But it wasn't up to her. Trent had made that much very clear. So, instead of following her instincts as a woman, she drew on her skills as a tough negotiator and tried one last time.

"That's all the more reason you should be the one to do the screenplay," she urged, appealing to his ego. "You can see that it's done exactly the way it should be done. I might even be able to get Trent to bend on giving you total creative control."

"Don't you understand yet?" Mark said, with an explosive fury that seemed to fill the air with electricity. A low growl rumbled in Shadow's throat and he inched protectively closer to Lindsay, just as Mark threw the contract back at her. It fluttered down onto Shadow's back.

"I don't give a damn about creative control," he shouted, then added with cold emphasis, "Listen to me closely. Read my lips if you have to: I do not want to see *Velvet Nights* done as a film at all."

Suddenly, with his sarcastic, biting words being hurled at her, Lindsay's frustration reached its limits. She was tired of being torn between her growing feelings for Mark and her obligations to Trent Studios. If she hadn't been so damned professional, she probably would have burst into tears. It was what she felt like doing. Instead, she lashed back at him.

"Then why in God's name did Morrie negotiate with us for the rights?" she demanded furiously. "The man's your agent. Not that I'd put it past him, but surely he wasn't running around making deals behind your back."

Mark gave her a wan smile. "You've met Morrie. He doesn't exactly listen, once you start talking in amounts over six figures. His eyes glaze over and he begins calculating his percentage."

Lindsay's eyes widened in amazement. "Then there was no bidding war among the studios?"

"Is that what he told Trent?"

"Of course. Trent wanted *Velvet Nights* very badly anyway, but hearing that a bunch of other studios wanted it as well made him crazy. He's obsessed with winning."

"Obviously Morrie knew that," Mark said dryly.

Lindsay was still trying to grasp the exact extent of Morrie's devious manipulations. "But you had told him the book wasn't up for grabs?"

"Approximately three thousand times," he confirmed. "But Trent Langston came after him and Morrie couldn't resist the action. Now he's trying to convince me to go along with it, to agree not only to selling the movie rights to Trent Studios, but to writing the screenplay as well."

He gazed directly into Lindsay's eyes, which were flashing sparks like an emerald held under a spotlight.

"Morrie and Langston both knew exactly how I felt," he said gently, which only increased her feeling of being had by a couple of scheming pros. "I had told them in language that would have curled your toes, just so there'd be no misunderstanding. They decided to give it another try anyway and picked you to come in here and make me change my mind. I guess they figured I'd be more susceptible to a pretty woman."

"And here I thought Trent selected me for my superb negotiating skills," she retorted dryly, knowing perfectly well that Mark was right on target. Trent had thought she'd use her feminine wiles to accomplish what he and Morrie hadn't been able to. He had, quite literally, thrown her out as bait. She'd have a few words to say to him about that when she got back to Los Angeles and, if Mark thought his language had been colorful, he should stop by and listen to the vocabulary she had in mind.

"It's nothing personal, bright eyes," Mark said more quietly. "They could have sent over the entire studio line-up of starlets and it wouldn't have made any difference. I don't want any part of this project.''

Lindsay studied him closely. One part of her responded to his obvious anguish, to his attempt even now to make sure that she hadn't taken his cutting barb or his rejection personally. It was the part of her that was falling in love with him, the part of her she was fighting a losing battle to ignore.

The part of her that worked for Trent Studios, the part that knew as well as anyone in the business how to cajole a reluctant actor or producer or writer into making a deal knew she was missing one critical piece of information, the piece that would make the whole puzzle fall into place and lead to a contract. What about *Velvet Nights* was making Mark Channing balk as he'd never done before over selling the rights to one of his bestsellers or writing the screenplay for it himself?

Even knowing that the issue was volatile and that she was risking his wrath by pursuing it, she decided to find that missing piece of information. She had to know—both professionally and, far more importantly, for herself and any future she hoped to have with him. The sudden, blink-of-an-eye discovery that she did want a future with this man astounded her, but it was not something she could take the time right now to explore. She had to get some more answers.

"Mark," she said softly. "Why does *Velvet Nights* mean so much to you? Why is it tearing you apart to even talk about it?"

His dark eyes widened and he regarded her incredulously. "Haven't you even read the damned book?"

She winced at the justifiably harsh condemnation in his tone. "No," she admitted reluctantly. "Trent sent me after you before I had a chance. He didn't even give me a copy."

Mark shook his head wearily, then got up slowly and went down the hall to his den. When he came back, he had the book in his hand. He gave it to her and said quietly, "When you've read it, we'll talk again. I'm going out for a while. I need some fresh air."

Lindsay watched him go out into the gathering twilight and howling wind with a heaviness in her heart. She had a feeling the two of them had lost something today, something elusive, rare and wonderful that had been within their grasp. She wondered wistfully if they'd ever be able to recapture the fragile trust, the easy camaraderie they'd built between them so quickly.

Then, determinedly pushing aside the futile, unanswerable questions that nagged at her, she settled comfortably on the sofa and opened *Velvet Nights*. From the first page of the thick volume she was absorbed by the tenderness, the emotional intensity and the gripping writing style that was so filled with imagery and love that she felt she knew the characters at once and shared their zany romance, their laughter and their wildly impetuous adventures. She could understand why Trent wanted this book so badly. It was an old-fashioned love story, filled with passion, an engaging humor and electric tension.

Lindsay hardly noticed when Mark came back, set a sandwich and cup of coffee beside her and went on to his own room. She was up the rest of the night reading the book and, when dawn broke through the darkness, she was huddled in a corner of the sofa, tears streaming down her face.

Her tears were not only for the characters in the book, but for Mark. She had realized almost from the outset that this had been a thinly veiled account of his own very special love story and when she reached the horribly tragic ending it wrenched her heart.

Reading the novel explained so much. His reluctance to see such personal intimacy played out on a movie screen. His quiet, solemn moods, when the world around him seemed to disappear. His understanding and compassion when she'd revealed her own childhood loss and admitted the effect it had had on her ability to love. Mark had suffered a similar, excruciatingly painful loss of someone he had loved very deeply and yet he had chosen to go on living. He wanted the same for her.

"What did you think?" he asked quietly, suddenly appearing in front of her. He was wearing faded, form-fitting jeans and another of those soft wool shirts, this one in an emerald green and black plaid that emphasized his own bold coloring. This morning, though, he looked pale and haggard, a shadow of a beard on his cheeks. She knew instinctively that he hadn't slept either.

"I'm sorry," she said softly. "I had no idea."

He shrugged. "You were just doing your job."

She shook her head. "I'm not sorry about that. I'm sorry about what happened. You must have loved her very much."

He nodded, his lips tightly compressed, his eyes haunted. "I did."

"Do you want to tell me about her?"

"It's all in the book."

"Not all of it, Mark," she retorted softly. "Remember what you said to me the other night: it can't be over, if it's still making you cry."

"I don't cry. Not anymore."

"Maybe not. But there's too much pain left in your eyes. I've seen it night after night, when I've walked down the hall to go to bed and left you sitting in here, staring into the fire. I'm seeing it again right now. Please, talk to me."

She paused, looked straight into his eyes and, after taking a deep breath, said quietly and with complete candor, "I love you, Mark, and I want to understand."

He didn't react to her words. It was almost as though she hadn't admitted at last that she loved him. If it hadn't been for the sorrow she saw in his eyes, she might have been hurt that he'd taken her admission so casually. Instead she simply waited.

Eventually he sank wearily down next to her and gazed blankly into the fire. Lindsay sat quietly, wanting to touch him, certain that she didn't dare. When the words finally began to come, they were jerky, awkward phrases, not at all like the glib chatter at which Mark was so good. Tumbling out, one after the other, taut with emotion, the words shed light where shadows had been in the book.

"I met Alicia in Switzerland. She was the gentlest, most sensitive woman I'd ever met. From the very first we were totally compatible. She understood my need to be alone and yet when we were together there was fire and passion and excitement and laughter.

"So much laughter," he recalled wistfully. "I don't think I ever saw her cry or make anyone else cry. She was always playing pranks, livening things up, issuing crazy challenges. She was Katharine Hepburn, Zelda Fitzgerald and the prom queen all rolled into one. There was nothing she wouldn't dare to do, no place she wouldn't go. We spent our winters in Switzerland, where I could write and she could ski, and in the summer we traveled. You can't begin to imagine what it was like."

Ironically, considering the depth of Mark's feelings, the still-raw emotions that talking about Alicia obviously aroused in him, Lindsay felt no sense of competitiveness. Sadly, what Mark and Alicia had shared was over now. Because of *Velvet Nights*, she could imagine what it must have been like for the two of them. She could see the beauty of it and, having just begun to feel the first stirrings of a deep love herself, she thought she had some idea of the depth of his suffering when it had ended.

"What really happened? Was it the way it was in the book?"

"Pretty much," he said curtly.

She touched him gently. "Would you rather not talk about it anymore?"

He hesitated, almost grasping at the reprieve she offered. "No," he said finally. "You were right. It's time to get it out. I thought the book had done that, but obviously I was wrong."

Lindsay waited and finally he went on.

"I was finishing up a manuscript one day. Alicia came into the den and said she was going skiing. She mentioned some trail that, if I'd been thinking about it, I would have realized was far too dangerous. She was good, but not that good. Unfortunately, I was so damned wrapped up in my work that I barely heard what she said.

"Sometime during the afternoon I began to get the strangest sensation that something was wrong, but I ignored it. I was on the last few pages and they were flowing like crazy. I wanted to finish so we could celebrate when Alicia got back."

He stood up and paced the room, prowling like a starving, half-crazed beast on a hunt, pain and anger written on his face, his lean body tense. Suddenly he slammed his fist down on a table, sending papers flying and tilting the lamp precariously.

"How could I have been so selfish, so damned blind?" he said, his voice raw and filled with self-recrimination. "If only I'd gone after her when I first had the feeling that something was wrong, maybe it would have made a difference."

Lindsay recalled his comment a few days ago about learning to trust his instincts. Now it was clear why there had been such intensity in what had seemed to be only a casual remark. One missing piece of the puzzle fell into place.

"What happened?"

"She got lost on the trail, at least that's what they think happened. What had started out as a light snowfall turned into a raging blizzard," he began, the haunted look making his eyes darker than ever, the words explaining his reaction to her disappearance from the cabin. Yet another piece of the puzzle clicked into place.

"Everyone else had come back to the lodge, but Alicia had wanted to do one more run. No one could talk her out of it. She dared the others to come with her, but they refused. As soon as they got back to town, they came to tell me she'd gone back up. I practically went out of my mind. I was furious with her friends for letting her go, but I knew they couldn't have stopped her. Not once she'd made up her mind. I wanted to go after her, but the snow was so bad by then, the official patrols wouldn't let me. We waited and waited and with every endless minute that passed, I knew that her odds of coming back were diminishing."

Mark's voice shook and he was barely controlling the sobs that shook his shoulders. "She died on that damn mountain, all alone."

Lindsay put her hand on his knee and he took it in his own and held it tightly. This time it was her turn to share her strength with him.

"I left Switzerland as soon as they found her. I buried her back in Vermont so she'd be near her family and then I bought this place. At first I was like a bear in hibernation. I refused to go out, to see anyone. Grace Tynan kept nudging at me until I finally pulled myself together. She didn't know what had happened, but she was determined not to let me hide away for the rest of my life."

His lips tilted in a crooked grin. "That woman's like a nagging old mother hen once she gets something in her mind. One day, after all that pushing and prodding, I just woke up and realized that whether I liked it or not, my life was going to go on. That was the day I started living again. It was also the day I started on the book.

"*Velvet Nights* is Alicia's story. It was something I had to tell to save my own soul, but I don't want to see it on a movie screen, twisted into some sentimental mockery of the way it really was with us."

Lindsay gazed into his troubled eyes and suggested softly, "You could make sure that didn't happen."

He shook his head. "I could, but I won't. It's been five years now and it's time to put Alicia to rest. I knew that the minute I first saw you and realized there were new possibilities, new feelings and that it was time I explored them."

She nodded, understanding at last at least some of what had been happening between them, certainly understanding how he felt about *Velvet Nights*.

"I'll tell Trent there is no deal," she said softly.

Their eyes met and held, hers filled with compassion and understanding, his filled with renewed life—and desire. Without a word being spoken, Lindsay went into his arms and offered him all of the love she had to give, more love than she'd ever thought herself capable of giving.

He held her cradled in his arms, his hands stroking tentatively, but building brushfires all the same. When his hand slipped under her sweater, his fingers warm and gentle against her already-burning flesh, her

breast tensed with anticipation, the nipple hardening.
When he touched it at last with a flick of his nail, an
exquisite spiral of electricity shot through her.

Through it all his eyes never left hers, and when
Lindsay wanted to look away, afraid to let him see her
vulnerability, her raw desire, a slight shake of his head
stopped her.

"I don't want your pity," he said softly.

"Pity is the last thing I'm feeling right now."

"Are you sure?"

The question seemed to carry a double meaning and
Lindsay's response was immediate and filled with
certainty. "Yes. I meant what I said before, Mark. I
love you."

Her lips parted ever so slightly in invitation, and
with a ragged sigh Mark took them, gently at first,
nibbling, teasing, until Lindsay felt an aching need stir
in her abdomen. When his tongue flicked across her
lips then slipped inside her mouth like liquid silk rippling across heated flesh, her whole body shuddered
and she clung to him.

"Oh, bright eyes, I need you so," he murmured as
his lips brushed across her cheeks, down her neck. His
fingers continued to tempt and tease each breast in
turn, the lacy fabric of her bra only adding to the de-
lightfully pleasurable friction of his touch. When his
hands moved on to roam over the curve of her hip, the
length of her legs, her breasts felt bereft, though she
hardly noticed because of the new tension he was
arousing wherever his fingers caressed.

She had never felt like this before, never known this
magical wonder of feeling her body come alive from

the inside, of feeling a heat that warmed like sunlight, then exploded into wicked flames that danced along her nerves. All of those unfamiliar yearnings she had felt from the moment she and Mark had met in the airport came into focus here and now in his arms, and she knew that he and he alone could fulfill every passionate dream that she'd ever had and tried so hard to deny.

She wanted to know this powerfully virile body that had drawn her into its forceful magnetic field. She wanted to touch every intriguing inch of rugged masculinity, to experience Mark's vitality as she had never experienced another man's. She wanted him to love her, to complete her in the mystical way that a man completes the woman he loves.

"Make love to me, Mark. Take me to your bed and make love to me."

He shook his head, his dark eyes burning into hers. "No, love. Here. I want to make love to you in the firelight. Your skin glows like pearls in this light," he said as he reached for her sweater and slipped it over her head. Her bra, jeans and panties followed in a slow, deliberately provocative stripping that had Lindsay trembling. When his hands skimmed over her now, caressing and stroking, her body arched into his touch, demanding more and more intensity, seeking satisfaction without knowing exactly when or how it would come.

She reached for Mark's clothes, trying to unbutton his shirt with shaking fingers, but he captured her hand and stilled it, sucking gently, provocatively on each fingertip. "Not yet," he whispered huskily. "Not yet."

His eyes were dark as night, so dark a woman could lose herself in them had it not been for the little pin-pricks of light that teased and taunted like guiding stars as his hands continued their erotic dance over her body. They glided slowly along her legs, paused intimately on her inner thigh and then, almost without warning, flicked across the tiny spot in which so much sensation seemed to be centered.

Lindsay's eyes widened at the contact and her hips began to move rhythmically as Mark's fingers played relentlessly across the moist, sensitive flesh. As spectacular as the sensation was, there was an aching emptiness that cried out to be filled. "Mark, please. I want you."

"Sssh. This is just for you," he said, intensifying his touch until Lindsay was no longer able to protest. "Let yourself go, bright eyes. That's it. I want you to feel everything."

Fire roared through her, exploding into a million colored lights as her body thrashed wildly beneath Mark's persistent fingers. There were no longer any thoughts of her one-sided vulnerability, no lingering hesitations about giving in to the all-consuming feelings. All rational thought was beyond her now as her body yielded itself to wondrous new sensations. It was only after the rippling waves of excitement calmed that she realized the extent of what Mark had given her. His eyes met hers and she saw that he knew exactly what she was thinking. What had she ever done to deserve a man whose one joy came in giving such pleasure? she wondered.

Lindsay turned to him then, and this time when she reached for the buttons of his shirt, he didn't deny her. She eased his clothes off in the same slow, enticing way he had removed hers, her eyes drinking in the sight of him, all sinew and potent strength. She struggled with his jeans then hesitated tentatively over the removal of his briefs, struck by a sudden uncertainty that vied at the same time with the desire that raged deep inside her once more.

Mark lifted his hips and slid off the pants that had only barely concealed his throbbing masculinity. Instinctively Lindsay's fingers sought him, reveling in the satin smoothness that shielded a core like white-hot steel. Mark trembled beneath her exploratory touches, his breathing growing increasingly ragged. When he reached for her at last, there was no holding back. They were two people whose needs were evenly matched, whose desires were beyond control. He poised above her only briefly, his gaze holding hers. For the tiniest fraction of a second Lindsay felt a flicker of fear, but it was banished almost before it could register completely in her mind.

She waited expectantly for Mark's first urgent thrust, then felt a sharp sting of pain that vanished almost as soon as it had begun. She saw the look of surprise in his eyes, the hesitancy, and deliberately arched her hips upward, drawing him into her, filling herself with him, reveling in the perfect fit of his body with hers. Slowly, they adjusted their rhythm and with each point and counterpoint, the tension built, coiling inside her like a spring, which once released would shake them both to their very cores. Mark's lips sought her breast and his tongue teased the hardened peak until Lindsay could feel the sensation clear down to the tips of her toes. Her fingers dug into his back, then slid down to his hips, pulling him more deeply into her until at last the spring snapped and her body shook with the explosiveness of the sensation.

Mark held perfectly still until her own shudders stopped, then he moved again and again, his muscles taut with tension until finally he, too, trembled, his body covered with a sheen of perspiration.

"I had no idea," they both said in a sort of dazed wonder.

"Why didn't you tell me?" he murmured, still holding her in his arms, their bodies curved together side by side.

"After everything I told you, I thought you knew."

"I suppose I should have guessed."

"Does it matter?"

"Yes. It matters."

Lindsay's face fell. "Why?"

"Not in that way, bright eyes. I'm just glad I'll always be the only man you've ever had."

"What does that mean?" she mumbled sleepily.

"Quiet, love. We'll talk about it later," he promised, as she settled her head more comfortably in the crook of his shoulder and promptly fell asleep. It was a sleep filled with spectacular dreams, and Mark was at the center of every one of them. With a wildfire of desire warming her from the inside, she didn't even seem to mind that they were always surrounded by snow.

Nine

Marry me," Mark suggested softly in the morning, his arms wrapped tightly around Lindsay, his breath whispering across her bare shoulder, his fingers delicately tracing the curve of her spine. "And if you say one word about this being so sudden, you're less perceptive than I thought you were."

Lindsay's heart turned a somersault, and she wished with everything that was in her that she could say yes. Somehow over the past few days she had fallen deeply, passionately in love with Mark Channing. She knew that with absolute certainty, had known it even before last night's tempestuous lovemaking that had bound her to him as irrevocably as the snare of a silken spider's web.

No man had ever made her feel as he had, as though the world were bright and clear and open to all sorts of new and exciting experiences to be shared. She had never known the joy of sharing before, never known what it was like to allow another human being to get so close that he seemed to be a part of her, seemed to know her thoughts practically before she spoke them aloud.

Mark had made her want to explore previously hidden facets of her personality, to seek out thrilling, new adventures. The man had even made skiing tolerable, for heaven's sakes! He must have a magic touch if he could make snow and icy arctic blasts of wind seem appealing. Well, she corrected, maybe not appealing exactly, but bearable.

But oddly, as certain as she was now of her own feelings, she wasn't at all sure he was in love with her. Not in the all-consuming, tender way he had loved Alicia. Deep inside she feared that she had just happened along at a time when Mark had decided to end his self-imposed isolation. Never once had he actually said he loved her. Though he had made love to her during the day and, after they had moved to his bed, on into the night with a passion and gentleness that went beyond thrilling to some extraordinary place of enchantment, that was not necessarily the same thing. Even his marriage proposal could have stemmed from loneliness and need, rather than love.

Besides, she told herself as she mentally built a case for resisting the very strong temptation to say yes, she was nowhere near ready to relinquish her own fear of commitment, not after so little time and especially not when she had so many uncertainties about his feelings. What if she lost him eventually? What on earth would she do then? She might be older and wiser than that nine-year-old child who'd suffered irreparable emotional harm over her father's sudden death, but she was no less vulnerable, no less likely to be torn apart inside.

"Have you fallen asleep on me?" he taunted. "It's not very flattering."

"No. I'm wide awake. If I hadn't been before, your proposal would have done it."

"Well, then, what's your answer?"

She hesitated, unable to bring herself to say either yes or no. "Couldn't we just sort of live together for a while?" she offered tentatively as an alternative, pushing aside the awareness that even that slender tie would put her emotions at tremendous risk. "I mean whenever we can work out something. I do have a job to get back to, after all."

He regarded her incredulously and his hands stilled in the middle of her back.

"How exactly do we *sort of* live together, if you're in Los Angeles and I'm here?"

"Actually I'm hardly ever in Los Angeles. I go all over the world."

"Which complicates things even more."

"Not really," she said, pursing her lips thoughtfully as she weighed the possibilities. "In the long run, that should help. Boulder is sort of in the middle between L.A. and anywhere."

"And you'll touch down whenever your route happens to carry you past?" There was an edge of sarcasm in his voice that she chose to ignore.

"Why not? Other people have commuter relationships."

"Usually when they can't sustain one at close range," he suggested dryly.

Lindsay winced, wondering how accurate the offhand remark might really be. She'd never really tried to sustain one at any distance. Still, she responded defensively, "That's not fair."

"But I'm hitting pretty close to the mark, aren't I? You're afraid to stay here with me full-time, married or not. You're afraid you'll start to care too much."

"I've already told you that I love you."

"Saying the words isn't enough. If you mean them, then make a commitment."

"It's too soon. Besides, you seem to have forgotten how I feel about this climate and the total isolation."

He leered at her suggestively and one hand slid slowly around until it was cupping her breast, his fingers playing gently with the tip until it tightened into a hard bud and a white-hot core of heat built deep within her. Lindsay gasped involuntarily as a whirlwind of sensations ripped through her anew.

"I've always thought isolation was a pretty good thing for newlyweds," he countered, continuing his sensual assault.

"It probably is...on a honeymoon," she conceded, trying to wriggle out of the path of his persistent, teasing fingers.

"Mark!" she said admonishingly.

"Yes."

"Stop it. You're not helping anything."

"I'm just trying to prove a point."

"So am I."

"Okay. I think I like mine better, but what's your point?" he asked grudgingly.

"That sooner or later we'll have to get back to real life and for you that means writing."

"So?"

"What am I supposed to do while you write? Sit in a rocker down at the general store next to Jeb and compare notes on the spring seed catalogs?"

"Of course not. You can work, if you want to."

"Fine. My job is based in Los Angeles and requires extensive traveling."

"I meant you could work here."

"Doing what?"

"I don't know. You're obviously an intelligent, talented woman. Check the papers."

"Oh, for crying out loud," she finally exploded in exasperation, jerking the sheet up and wrapping it protectively around her so he could no longer distract her with his roving touch. "I already have a career."

Mark shrugged indifferently. "I'm not convinced you're that crazy about it."

His casual words struck a responsive chord in her and Lindsay wondered if he weren't closer to the truth than she'd ever admitted to herself. Maybe she'd only been trying to prove something to herself with this crazy job that took her to the ends of the earth and back again, never giving her a minute to herself. Well, she'd been up in more planes than she could count over the last few years, and while she hadn't exactly conquered her fear of flying, at least she'd learned to live with it.

As for the job itself, was she tired of it? Had she only been using it as an excuse to avoid involvements? Even if she had, she decided stoutly, Mark was not going to force her into making a decision she wasn't ready to make and she was definitely not prepared to make this one, no matter how strongly she felt about him.

She glowered at him and muttered, "That's not for you to decide."

Mark sighed. "No. I don't suppose it is. Maybe we should make another deal."

Lindsay regarded him doubtfully. He was obviously even better at this "deal" business than she was. The last one he'd offered had gotten her in way over her head. Another one would probably send her under for the third time. "What's the deal?" she asked cautiously.

"We'll try it your way for one month."

"A month?" she repeated incredulously. "That's no deal. You know the kind of work I do. I may be in Cannes or New York or L.A. for the next month."

"Then it won't work out very well, will it?"

"Are you trying to set me up to lose?"

"No, of course not," he said innocently, though there was a wicked glimmer in his eyes when he added, "but if it doesn't work out, we'll try it my way."

"Exactly what is your way?" she asked skeptically.

"We'll get married."

They seemed to be right back where they'd started. "How will that solve anything? I'll still be traveling."

"No, you won't. That's part of the deal. You'll stay here with me."

"Damn it, Mark. Haven't you heard anything I've said?"

"I've heard all of it."

"And what it comes down to is that you expect me to make a choice between you and my career?"

"Why not? What would you do if you fell in love with someone who lived in Bangor, Maine? Would you expect to commute, would you leave your job or would you dump him?"

"Oh, don't be absurd. I don't even know anyone in Maine."

"You didn't know anyone in Boulder until a few days ago. Now that you do, maybe it's time to sort through your priorities."

"If that's not the most arrogant, chauvinistic statement I've ever heard in my life," she exclaimed. "Who are you to question my priorities? Why should I give up my career, move to a place where you freeze to death in anything less than four layers of clothing and sit around all day staring at the walls, while you lock yourself away in another room and write to your heart's content? What's wrong with you making a few compromises? You could write anywhere."

"That's true," he admitted slowly. "I could. But I hate Los Angeles and you said yourself you're never there anyway."

"So get a portable typewriter. You can sit next to me and write on the plane."

"Very funny."

"Well, it's no more absurd than you asking me to give up everything," she snapped, then sighed wearily. "Look, this is getting us nowhere. You don't want to live in Los Angeles. I don't want to live in Boulder. You apparently want me at your beck and call. I need my independence. Sounds to me like any judge would agree we've got a good case for irreconcilable differences."

"Gosh," he said with a wicked grin. "We're not even married and you're already throwing around divorce court terms."

"I might as well start practicing. Can't you see this would never work?"

"Of course it would."

"If I give in."

"Only on one or two points."

"They're pretty big points. Exactly how are you planning to bend?"

"Well..."

"I thought so."

Suddenly he gave her one of those full-blown, dazzling, dimpled smiles that had gotten her into this emotional clench in the first place. "Am I mistaken or somewhere in the middle of all this did you agree to the basic idea of marrying me?" he asked.

"Of course not."

"Then why are we battling over where we're going to live after we're married?"

She grinned back at him tentatively. "Because it's a safer topic?"

"That's what you think. You haven't heard all of the awful, rotten things I can say about Los Angeles. Do you actually want your children to grow up in a place where they can't see the mountains for the smog?"

"Do you want them to grow up where it'll take an hour for them to thaw out their little hands?"

"Now we're getting somewhere," he said enthusiastically.

Lindsay looked at him blankly. "Where?"

"We're discussing this rationally."

"You call this rational?"

"Well, in a twisted sort of way it is."

She shook her head. "I think that's the problem. Your mind's warped from all this damp weather."

"Would you rather just talk about getting married? I can do that."

"What's the point?"

"We love each other."

"We do?"

"I love you," he said emphatically and with such absolute conviction that it rocked Lindsay back on her heels. She dropped the sheet and simply stared at him. Mark's eyes immediately lowered to take in her firm breasts. The warm appreciation in his gaze sent a ripple of excitement skittering along her spine.

"You do?"

"Well, of course. I wouldn't have asked you to marry me otherwise." He looked at her oddly. "What did you think?"

"I thought maybe you were just tired of being out here all by yourself, which," she added significantly,

"I could certainly understand. This place makes me crazy and I've only been here a few days."

He shook his head as though trying to clear it. "Let me get this straight. You think that just because I'm tired of being stranded out here all alone, I asked a woman who wants to wander the globe to marry me? That doesn't make a lot of sense."

"None of this makes any sense. I came here to get you to sign a simple movie deal and now you're trying to negotiate a marriage contract. The role reversal has my head spinning."

"Good. I like to keep my women off balance."

"Your *women*!"

"I meant my woman. You." He tried to kiss her, but she ducked out of reach. "Only you, Lindsay. I swear."

"Right. Exactly how often do you propose?"

"You're the first," he said, suddenly sobering. "Since Alicia."

"Oh, Mark," she murmured, instantly apologetic. She slid her arms around him, her breasts brushing against his chest. "I'm sorry."

"There's no need for you to be sorry," he said huskily. "Just marry me."

"I can't," she said insistently.

To her utter astonishment, Mark freed himself from her embrace and casually jumped out of bed.

"Okay," he said easily, striding toward the bathroom, thoroughly at ease with his magnificent nakedness. Her pulse danced a dramatic tango at the sight of him.

"Okay?" she murmured, unable to tear her eyes off of his muscular frame.

"Sure. We'll go see Grace. She'll be able to talk you into it," he said confidently.

"Mark Channing, this is between you and me. If you can't talk me into it, no one can."

"You just wait until you hear Grace try. She's very determined to marry me off. She's just been waiting for the right candidate to come along."

Lindsay sighed as the bathroom door shut behind him. Grace Tynan was indeed very determined and her own resistance was weakening with every minute that passed. But she was not going to rush recklessly into a commitment that she might regret the rest of her life. She might not have a lot of experience in such matters, but she knew perfectly well that no one in her right mind would decide to get married five days after meeting someone in an airport newsstand, even if he did have dazzling dimples and a sharp, irreverent mind that made hers spark and crackle just to keep up with it. They might have a rip-roaring, spectacularly satisfying affair, but that was the most that could possibly come of such a passionate, short-term encounter.

She picked up a pillow that was fragrant with Mark's masculine scent and hugged it to her. An affair was the most that could happen, wasn't it? she thought desperately.

An hour later, they were trudging through the snow toward the general store, Lindsay's mittened hand held in Mark's gloved one. Despite all that interference, she could feel the warmth of his touch flashing right straight through her. She was hardly even aware that the wind-chill factor was somewhere below zero and the snow drifts on the side of the road were up to her chin. Mark's unsettling ability to make her forget her surroundings was not a good omen for a woman who was trying to resist a proposal.

When they reached the store and threw open the door, Grace and Jeb greeted them with welcoming smiles. The pair quickly took in the fact that Lindsay's hand was firmly grasped in Mark's and their eyes lit with the approval of a couple of dedicated matchmakers.

"Howdy, you two," Jeb bellowed enthusiastically. "Get in here and get that door shut. It's colder outside than a witch's..."

"Jeb!" Grace thundered warningly, then beamed at them. "Sit down. I'll get some tea. Or would you rather have hot chocolate?"

"Oh, hot chocolate sounds wonderful," Lindsay sighed. "If it's not too much trouble."

"Not a bit. It's Mark's favorite too."

Lindsay caught the triumphant gleam in his eye. He actually considered their mutual desire for hot chocolate a point in his favor on the unevenly tipped scale of their romance. He apparently figured Lindsay and Grace would grasp the significance of it, too.

"So, what brings you two out from in front of a warm fire?" Jeb asked. "Just come down to get the mail, did you?"

"Not exactly," Mark said. "I want Grace to do something for me."

"What's that?" she called from the back room.

"I want you to propose to Lindsay for me," he said perfectly calmly, as Jeb suddenly hooted wildly and slapped his knee.

"Hey, Grace! Did you hear that? This ought to be a good one," he snickered. He settled back in his rocker and watched them expectantly.

"Mark!" Lindsay protested weakly as embarrassment flooded through her.

"Well," Mark retorted defensively, "that's what we came down here for."

"We did not. We came to visit."

"Maybe you came to visit. I came to get Grace to propose to you."

Grace poked her head around the doorway. "Any reason you can't do your own proposing, young man?" she inquired sternly.

"She won't listen to me."

"Then what on earth makes you think she'd listen to me?"

"I thought you could tell her about my finer points, sort of act as my agent."

"Don't mention agents," Lindsay said with a shudder. "If you get Morrie in on this, I'll walk out on you for sure."

"No Morrie," he agreed. "I think this needs a woman's touch. Come on, Grace. You can do it."

"I'm thinking the girl must have a pretty good reason for saying no to a man like you. She's been locked away in the cabin all alone with you for days now. She's probably seen a side of you the rest of us don't know about. Maybe she doesn't love you."

"Of course, she loves me," Mark retorted indignantly. "She's just being stubborn."

"Stubborn!" Lindsay said indignantly. "I am not being stubborn. I am just trying to preserve life as I know it."

"What's that mean?" Jeb wanted to know.

"It means she doesn't like cold weather," Mark answered.

"Don't blame her much. My bones are beginning to take a mighty strong dislike to all these howling winds too."

"Your bones are a lot older than hers, you old coot," Grace barked, as she brought in a tray with steaming mugs of hot chocolate. "Besides, ain't nobody stopping you from moving to Arizona or Florida, if that's what you want."

"You won't go."

"Of course, I won't go. I like it here. What's that got to do with anything?"

"You blasted well know I'm not going anywhere without you, Grace Tynan, not after all these years."

"Then settle back and hold your arthritic old hands over the stove and keep your mouth shut. Let Mark and Lindsay try to work this out."

"Seems to me they're not doing too well on their own, if they had to come down here to get you to run interference," Jeb shot back.

"You, of all people," he added in disgust.

"What's that supposed to mean, Jeb Davis?" Grace demanded, her blue eyes flashing dangerously.

"Just that you ought to be paying a little more attention to your own life and not worrying about everyone else's."

"He might have a point there," Mark said helpfully, as Grace glared at him.

"Mark Channing, unless you want me to tell this woman to run for her life, you'd best not be siding with Jeb."

"Oh, are there two different sides here?" he asked innocently. "I was kind of hoping you two were on the same one."

"In a pig's eye," Grace sniffed. "We're getting off the subject anyway. If you want Lindsay to marry you, then you're just going to have to convince her you love her."

"She knows I love her."

"And you're sure she loves you?"

Lindsay was beginning to get the feeling that neither of them remembered that she was around. Jeb shrugged and gave her a sympathetic, I-know-what-you're-up-against look.

"Of course, she loves me. I've already told you that."

"Then what's the problem?"

"The problem," Lindsay interrupted emphatically, "is that your pigheaded friend here expects me to do all of the compromising."

"Ahh. I see. Like what?"

"Like giving up my career and moving here to flounder around in snow up to my knees."

"There's no snow in the summer," Mark pointed out cheerfully.

"Then let's just live here in the summer," she countered.

"Good," Grace said approvingly. "Now that's a compromise."

"But I love it here in the winter," Mark said plaintively.

Lindsay threw up her hands. "See what I mean?"

"Yes. I think I do." Grace scowled at Mark. "Which do you love more: winters in Boulder or Lindsay?"

Lindsay chuckled as she watched the play of expressions on Mark's face. "Shoe's on the other foot now, isn't it?" she said gleefully.

"Yes," he conceded grudgingly.

"How's it feel?"

"It's damned uncomfortable."

Lindsay gave Grace a grateful look. "Thank you."

"Anytime."

She gazed into Mark's troubled eyes. "Want to go back now?"

"Why not?" he said, his tone suddenly defeated. "I suppose you'll want to leave now."

"Yes," she said softly, her eyes catching his, her lips curving into a slow, easy smile. "I think it's time I started packing."

"Okay. Let's go."

"Of course," she said, gazing at him impishly, "I didn't bring all that much."

Mark's eyes lit up. "So?"

"I suppose it could wait until morning."

Ten

It was a long, long time until morning and Mark filled every minute with incredible tenderness and spellbinding passion. Lindsay had nothing to compare it with, but she knew intuitively that what was happening between them was unique, that she would capture this sort of wildly sensuous responsiveness and wanton abandonment with no other man.

As dawn approached, Lindsay could read the sadness in Mark's eyes, knew that it was reflected in her own, but they had talked for hours and eventually she had been able to make him see that it was too soon for unwilling compromises. They had come together for an explosive moment in time and now they needed time apart to sort things out. They each had to find their own way back into each other's arms.

"You know that once you leave, it will be that much harder for you to come back," Mark said as he sat propped up in bed and watched her pack the few things she had brought with her for what had been meant to be nothing more than a brief business trip, but had turned into an unbelievably romantic, once-in-a-lifetime experience.

"Not if it's right," she countered. "If we were meant to be, we'll find a way to make it work. And if we weren't, then..."

She found she couldn't complete the thought because the idea of not spending the rest of her life with Mark suddenly terrified her. Already the thing she had feared most had happened. She was captivated by an intriguing man and no amount of distance and perspective was likely to change that. She wanted to run straight back into his arms, to snuggle next to him under the covers and feel the crisp hairs on his chest as they taunted her bare skin, to feel his warmth and strength and love surround her with an astounding beauty. She wanted to stay there and never let him go.

But she knew it would be wrong. If they didn't work out their differences about the future in a way that was right for both of them they would make each other miserable in the end. And there had to be a way to do that, she reassured herself. There had to be! Two people as in love as they were could not be kept apart.

The drive to the airport seemed to take forever over roads made hazardous by a fresh coating of ice. Mark's hands gripped the wheel with white-knuckled intensity and Lindsay knew it was not entirely due to the condition of the highway. He hated letting her go even more than she hated leaving. The tension in his body had told her that—from the instant they had left Jeb and Grace the previous night. Even at the height of passion, there was no emotional release for him. Instead, there had been only a growing sorrow and desperation that had made each taking of her willing body more urgent. There had been exciting peaks of violent, soul-shaking shudders, but no aftermath of calm.

At the airport Mark left her alone at the check-in counter for several minutes. She was still in line when a familiar, beloved hand reached over her shoulder and held out a chocolate bar and a bag of chocolate-covered almonds. Lindsay turned and gave him a wobbly grin and felt sudden tears well up in her eyes. She tried to blink them away before he could see them, but she was too late. He brushed away the single tear that had escaped and rolled down her cheek.

"Don't go," he urged softly.

"I have to."

Her hand reached out to caress his cheek, lingering at the spot where a smile would create one of his beloved dimples. Except there was no smile now and he trembled visibly beneath her touch.

"You don't have to. You want to."

"Mark, we've been all through this. We need time. Things happened too fast. You're asking me to make changes in my life I'm not ready to make. Commitment. A move. Giving up my career. A few days ago those ideas were the farthest things from my mind. I couldn't have imagined, then, ever loving anyone the way I love you."

"And now that you do?"

"I need time to figure out what to do about it and so do you. I can't be the only one to make concessions. It's going to take compromises from both of us to make this work."

"Just don't forget about me," he said and there was such vulnerability in his voice that Lindsay was touched beyond measure.

"How could I ever forget about you?" she teased gently. "You taught me to ski."

He grinned and the fleeting hint of a dimple taunted her. "At the time, you didn't consider that a point in my favor."

"Maybe in time I will," she said, sliding her arms around his waist, molding her body into the fit of his, trying to absorb the scent and feel of him, so that the memories would last for however long they were separated. "I do love you, Mark."

He kissed her then, his lips hard and urgent against hers, his tongue seeking, demanding a promise that she could not give him verbally. Her body gave it to him, though. Her senses yielded to his questing lips, wanting him yet again after a night that had been filled with so much loving.

Then reluctantly, when she wanted most to stay, she turned and walked away, trying to still the sobs that threatened to overcome her and reveal the depth of her own vulnerability.

Once she was on the plane, Lindsay tried to convince herself that time and perspective would lessen the intensity of what she had found with Mark, that while she might go on loving him, just as she had assured him she would, there would no longer be this horrible, aching need inside her. She was sure that once she was caught up in her old life, the memories would fade, lose their allure and give her peace again.

Except it didn't work out quite that way.

After only a few days back on the job, she discovered that she missed Mark as she had never missed the traveling and hotel rooms and late-night meetings that she'd left behind during her stay in Boulder. While she didn't miss the snow exactly, she found herself thinking longingly of those cozy hours in front of the fire with Mark's arms securely around her, the love in his eyes caressing her until she, too, felt a blazing warmth.

Mark's frequent calls, the long, midnight conversations that ended with sleepy good nights and murmured words of love only taunted her. It took nearly a month before she finally admitted the truth: that it was too late to avoid commitment and, even if it weren't, independence and freedom from the fear of loss were not a fair exchange for the man she had come to love so deeply. Even sunshine and warm breezes didn't matter without the right person to share them. Every bed she slept in on her increasingly frequent business trips seemed lonelier than ever before.

And yet she knew that she couldn't do as he expected and simply walk away from everything she had worked so hard to achieve. She had found that she did love her work, that what she'd been missing was balance, and with Mark she had found that balance. Her work was challenging and satisfying, even when it was thoroughly frustrating and Trent was his most maddening, as he had been ever since her return.

Just as she'd predicted, he had sulked upon learning that she'd failed to sign Mark to do *Velvet Nights*, but apparently he'd sensed that something had happened during that trip because he quickly tempered his disappointment and began giving her more and more work to do. Each new assignment carried more responsibility accompanied by demanding deadlines that allowed no time for long hours of soul-searching, much less for those longed-for stopovers in Boulder.

Worse, Mark hadn't even invited her to come back, and the fact that he hadn't even suggested a visit created an aching emptiness inside Lindsay that wouldn't go away. At first she'd been sure that pride stood in his way, but as time went on, she wasn't so certain. Maybe for Mark the past few weeks had proven the truth of her statement that during a separation they might discover that theirs was a love that was fleeting, a love that was never meant to be. Unfortunately, for her it had proven just the opposite.

On Monday morning, after spending a lonely, depressing, rainy weekend in her apartment catching up with her bills and her laundry, Lindsay arrived at work and found an urgent message from Trent waiting on her desk. Since all of Trent's messages were urgent, she debated ignoring it, but finally she gave in, went up to his penthouse office suite and tapped on the door.

"Who is it?" he barked with his usual lack of congeniality. He hated it when his secretary left her desk, yet he persisted in sending her on errands that took her from one end of the studio lot to the other.

Lindsay sighed and opened the door. Judging from his tone, it was going to be one of those days.

"What's up?"

"I need you to get to New York right away," he instructed without preamble.

"But I just got back from New York Friday night," Lindsay protested wearily. She'd been counting on spending most of the week right here in town.

"Janice booked you on the ten-thirty flight," he continued as though she'd never opened her mouth. "You've got a dinner meeting with Morrie. He thinks David Morrow might be wavering."

"Oh, dear Lord," she groaned. "Not this again."

"Lindsay!"

"David Morrow is not wavering," she retorted emphatically. "Morrie's just too greedy to know when to give up. And if you think I'm going to start crisscrossing this continent in pursuit of a deal that will never happen, you're out of your mind."

He regarded her quizzically. "You have another job in mind?"

"No. I do not have another job in mind. This one suits me just fine." She scowled at him fiercely. "Most of the time."

"Good. Then you'd better get moving. You've only got two hours to catch your plane."

He was obviously unimpressed by her outburst. She tried again.

"I'm not going. I know Mark—David Morrow—is not going to sell us the rights to *Velvet Nights*. Period. End of negotiations. Fini. Have I gotten through to you yet?"

"The question is, have I gotten through to you? I want you in New York tonight, sitting down to a lovely dinner with Morrie, working out the details of this deal.''

''The only thing I'll be doing at dinner with Morrie is breaking his knuckles when he tries to grab my leg. The man's like an octopus.''

''Lindsay!'' Trent growled impatiently.

''Okay,'' she said at last, throwing up her hands in defeat. ''I'll go, if it'll make you happy, but you're wasting the airfare.''

He shrugged. ''I own stock in the airlines.''

''I should have known.''

Nearly twelve tiring hours later she was sitting in a pleasant, exclusive French restaurant with Morrie, debating between coq au vin and veal *à la française*. She had managed successfully to inch her chair well out of the reach of his roaming hands and had placidly ignored his lecherous glances. She was going to enjoy this dinner from escargots to cherries jubilee, if she had to ask the maître d' to seat her at a separate table.

Unfortunately, before she could place her order the waiter came over with a telephone, plugged it in and said, ''For you, mademoiselle.''

''Me?''

''You are Mademoiselle Tabor?''

''Yes.''

''Then it is for you. Long distance.''

Lindsay picked up the phone, expecting to hear Trent's voice. It would not be unlike him to call right in the middle of dinner just to see how things were progressing. Instead, it was Mark who growled at her, ''What the hell are you doing in New York again?''

"Nice to hear from you, too," she murmured sweetly.

"I thought you told me you were going to be in Los Angeles most of the week."

"I was, but Trent had other ideas. I'm having dinner with a friend of yours."

"Morrie?" he asked incredulously.

"Who else? The two of them seem to think you're wavering."

"Like hell. Put him on."

She turned to Morrie, who was rapidly turning pale beneath his sunlamp tan. "Your client would like to speak to you."

Lindsay couldn't hear exactly what Mark was saying, even though he was shouting. As for Morrie's end of the conversation, it consisted mostly of mumbled apologies and incomplete sentences. It did her a world of good to see him at a loss for words. Finally, a defeated expression on his face, he handed the phone back to her.

"How long will you be in New York?" Mark asked.

"Another day or so."

"You're sure?" he persisted.

"As sure as I can ever be working for Trent. He had a couple of other things he wanted me to check out while I was here. Why?"

"I miss you, that's all," he said vaguely.

"I miss you, too," she replied softly, lowering her voice so that Morrie couldn't hang on every word. "More than I can say."

"Bye, bright eyes. Take care of yourself."

"Night, love."

After the call, Morrie behaved as though he were out with his dearest sister. He couldn't have been more polite or thoughtful. Lindsay wondered exactly what Mark had said to turn the groping monster into a docile lamb. He left her at her hotel with a handshake and an effusive apology for dragging her all this way for nothing.

"I'll call Trent myself and explain," he offered.

"Good idea," Lindsay replied. "Better he should burn your ears than mine."

"Good night, kiddo," he said with a jaunty voice. "If the writer starts giving you a rough time, you can always come back to me."

"I'll keep that in mind," she said as she walked away.

When she picked up her messages at the desk, she noted that there were three from Trent, each sounding increasingly urgent. This time she followed her instincts. She tossed them in the trash, took a shower and went to bed.

Twenty minutes later she was awakened by the shrill ring of the phone.

"'Lo," she mumbled.

"Lindsay, is that you?"

The sound of Trent's voice snapped her awake. "Of course, it's me. Who'd you expect to find in my room?"

"Why didn't you return my calls?"

"I didn't want to."

"You didn't want to! What do you think I pay you for?" His voice rose in a shriek, then fell again.

"Never mind. Just get on the first plane out of there in the morning and get back here."

Lindsay moaned and buried her head under the pillow. "Trent, what's going on now? I barely got off a plane. I thought you wanted me to see those advertising people tomorrow and interview that guy who's applying for the legal department."

"That can wait. I need you back here."

"What's so all-fired important that it can't wait a few days?"

"Morrow's in town."

Lindsay sat straight up in bed. The pillow toppled onto the floor. "He's what?"

"He's in town. I saw him in a restaurant tonight. Get back here and maybe you can wrap this whole thing up."

"There is nothing to wrap up."

"What does that mean? Didn't you and Morrie settle the details?"

"There were no details to settle. You'll be getting a call from Morrie in the morning. He'll explain."

"I want you to explain," he retorted. "No. Forget explaining. Just get back here and set up something with Morrow." He slammed the phone down before she could respond.

Lindsay was awake half the night after that trying to figure out what Mark was doing in Los Angeles and why he hadn't told her he was there when he called. Whatever the reason, she had absolutely no hesitation in the morning about following Trent's latest barrage of orders. In fact, she could hardly wait to carry them out.

She was at the airport well before flight time, anxious to get back to L.A. and into Mark's arms. She was so busy checking her watch every five minutes throughout the trip that she hardly even noticed she was on a plane. It was the only time that had ever happened except for the flight she'd taken with Mark at her side.

When she got to Trent Studios just after lunchtime, she riffled impatiently through her messages, certain there would be one from Mark. Surely he'd called her there first yesterday. That was the only way he could have found out where she was last night. There was no message and although her secretary recalled talking to him and giving him her New York itinerary, she said he hadn't said a word about being in Los Angeles.

Disappointed, Lindsay went into her office and sat down at her desk. Now what? He did have an answering service in Boulder. Surely they would know how to reach him. Quickly she picked up the phone and dialed, only to have the girl on the other end of the line tell her that she had no idea where Mr. Channing was.

"I'm sure he'll be calling in, though, if you'd like to leave a message."

"Just tell him that Lindsay called. He can reach me at my office."

It was nearly two hours later, when her secretary buzzed her and announced that Mark was on the line. She poked the blinking light without even saying thank you.

"Hi."

"Hi, yourself," he responded in a tone that was less than enthusiastic. In fact, he sounded exceedingly tired and very short-tempered. "I thought you were going to be in New York a couple of days."

"I was, but Trent found out you were here and ordered me home. Why didn't you tell me you were in Los Angeles when I talked to you last night?"

"It hardly seemed relevant, since you were clear across the country."

"Well, I'm back now. I don't suppose I could talk you into a nice, quiet dinner at this cozy little place I know of," she suggested in a low, sensuous voice designed to lure any male straight into a feminine snare. "It has a terrific view and the cook's not bad."

"Sounds tempting."

"Well?"

"Unfortunately, I'm in New York."

"You're where?"

"New York. I thought I'd surprise you."

Lindsay groaned in frustration. "Well, you've certainly done that."

"Exactly how long do you expect to be in L.A. this time?"

"Until Trent finds out you're in New York, I suppose."

"Don't tell him a thing," he said urgently. "And do not, whatever you do, get on another plane in the next twenty-four hours. I don't care if you can get a deal on the Taj Mahal as a backdrop for an action-adventure blockbuster. Stay put."

"Any particular reason?" she teased lightly.

"I have plans for you."

"Sounds interesting. Want to tell me about them?"

His voice dropped to a husky rumble. "Oh, I think you'll find they'll be worth your time."

"What do I do if Trent wants me to chase after you?"

"Tell him a smart woman never chases a man."

"Oh, is that so? Did you learn that at your grandmother's knee?"

"No. At my father's. He told me all about my mother's tricks. She played very hard to get."

"What exactly does that have to do with our situation?"

"Not much, but it may keep Trent in limbo for a day or two while he thinks about it."

"Trent doesn't like being in limbo. He pays me to chase people."

"Tell him that only results in two people running around in circles. We're living proof of that."

"I'm not sure he'll buy that argument."

"You can sell it to him, sweetheart. You're the best he's got."

"I couldn't sell you on the *Velvet Nights* deal."

"Not for lack of trying," he said with a dry chuckle. "Now will you stay put until I get there or not?"

"I will be waiting right here."

"Not right there," he corrected. "I want you at home, in something sleek and sexy."

"Any particular meal I should have on the stove?"

"If you play your cards right, we won't have time for food."

"I'll remind you of that when you're rummaging around in my empty refrigerator."

"Well, you might pick up a bottle of wine."

"And a loaf of bread?" she taunted.

"It'll be enough for me," he said and she could picture those dimples of his dipping into his cheeks as he grinned wickedly. "What about you?"

"I think I'll buy a few other things just in case."

"Lindsay."

"Yes."

"I love you."

"I love you, too."

"We're going to make this work."

"If you say so," she said, her voice still edged with doubts.

"I say so. I have the final chapter all written."

"Unfortunately real life isn't quite as easy to manipulate as the characters in a book."

"It is if you want something badly enough, and I want you, bright eyes," he whispered, his voice husky with promise. "See you soon."

Lindsay gently put the receiver back on the hook and sat back, her expression dreamy. Maybe their story would have a happy ending after all. At the very least, she could hardly wait to see what happened next.

Eleven

——

Lindsay took the stairs up two flights to Trent's office. When she walked in, she found his winded secretary slumped down in the chair behind her desk, her shoulders sagging, her face just a shade lighter than fire-engine red, her brown eyes flashing angry sparks.

"I swear one of these days, as soon as I catch my breath, I'm going to kill that man," Janice muttered ferociously.

"What's he done now?"

"The usual. I just got back from taking papers clear across the lot to be signed by the producer of one of those sitcoms for the fall and now our beloved boss wants me to trot back across to pick them up."

"Why didn't you just wait while you were there?"

"Because the man was not in his office and Mr. Langston wanted me back here 'immediately!'" She mimicked his authoritarian tone precisely.

"Why? What was so urgent?"

"Dictation, which, by the way, is what I thought he was hiring me to do when I took this job. Hasn't anyone ever explained to him that running errands is precisely why he maintains a very large messenger crew?"

Lindsay grinned at the plaintive note in her voice. Janice had only been there two months. The previous secretary had lasted less than a week. She'd quit in a rage after making fifteen trips in a single morning. As she'd stormed out the door, she'd been mumbling something about joining a health club, if she wanted exercise.

"We've all tried, but those are for ordinary messages. Mr. Langston's messages are not ordinary," she advised with mock severity. "They cannot be trusted to the simple folk. They are so top secret I'm surprised he hasn't trained an entire fleet of carrier pigeons to fly them to their destinations."

"Why should he do that when he has me?" Janice grumbled. "By the way, if you want to see him, go on in. I'm not saving his hide from anybody today."

Lindsay chuckled and walked in.

"I thought I sent you on an errand," Trent groused without looking up.

"No. That was Janice," Lindsay said sweetly. "You sent me on another wild-goose chase."

His head jerked up and he beamed at her, those perceptive, crystal blue eyes of his scanning her from head to toe. "You're back. Terrific. What's the story? Have you made contact with Morrow yet? When are you meeting with him? I want this deal, Lindsay."

"So you've said."

"Well?"

"I just wanted you to know that I'm taking the rest of the week off," she announced blithely, giving him her cheeriest smile and watching his joviality vanish like a puff of smoke. She had a feeling it was a moment she would treasure always.

"Oh, no, you're not," he roared. "You're supposed to be setting up a meeting with Morrow."

"Oh, I will be seeing Mr. Morrow," Lindsay replied airily as she retreated right back out the door.

Trent beamed. "Well, why didn't you say so? Take all the time you want," he said, suddenly gracious again. She groaned at the turnaround. Oh, how he loved the role of benevolent dictator! She had an irresistible urge to prick his rapidly ballooning ego. She poked her head back in the door.

"One thing you should know, though," she added. Trent looked at her expectantly. "This meeting is strictly personal."

"Like hell!" She could still hear the rumble of his swearing as she ran down the steps chuckling to herself. She stopped by her office to pick up her purse— no briefcase this time, she thought defiantly—and took the elevator downstairs.

An hour later she had finished a whirlwind shopping binge that included buying the sexiest lingerie she had ever owned. She had also picked up enough groceries to satisfy two starving people for a week. She had no idea when Mark would get in or how long he would stay, but she intended to be prepared for the start of a lifetime, if that's what he had in mind.

She put a bottle of wine on ice, soaked in a bubble bath, put so much cream on her skin she practically skidded out of bed and went to sleep.

It was the middle of the night when she finally heard the buzz of her doorbell. Wrapping a satin and lace concoction around her nude body, she peeked out and saw Mark leaning back against the opposite wall. He looked beat. He also looked very, very desirable, which answered one question she'd had for the past few weeks. *That* had not changed.

"Hi, mister," she drawled sexily, after opening the door a crack. "Been in town long?"

"Thank God," he murmured fervently, as she gave him a puzzled look. "You're actually here. I don't think I could have taken one more flight."

She grinned at him. "I'm here. Are you coming in or has your energy run out?"

His gaze roved over her then and his eyes darkened with a smoldering sensuality. "I think I've just been rejuvenated. Do you have anything on under that?" he asked, eyeing her curiously.

Lindsay tilted her head provocatively and gave him a teasing smile. "Not a thing."

Mark groaned, pushed himself away from the wall and took three long strides toward her. Then she was in his arms, as he kicked the door shut behind him and lowered his face to taste her lips, taking them with the hungry urgency of a man too long denied. His hands glided over her slim, satin-covered body, inflaming her. Her tongue met his, teasing, taunting and then retreating. His mouth burned against her throat as he tasted her heated flesh, then cooled it with a gentle lapping of his tongue that made her tremble in his embrace.

Lindsay's breath caught in her throat as he undid the belt of the robe and slid it slowly off her shoulders. The material flowed to her feet, caressing as it went, landing in a satiny pool of aqua edged in white lace.

"I want you, bright eyes," he murmured against the creamy flesh of her breast. "I want you."

Lindsay arched back against the brace of his arm, waiting for his lips to capture her rapidly hardening nipples, but the desired touch didn't come. She opened heavy-lidded eyes and looked at him, suddenly realizing that the man was half asleep on his feet. Subduing her own disappointment and rapidly escalating libido, she curved a supporting arm around his waist.

"Come with me. I think it's time you had some sleep."

"I want to make love to you," he protested, but it was a weak argument.

"Later, love. We have all the time in the world."

She barely got him out of his shirt and jeans before he collapsed across the bed . . . diagonally. She stood surveying him and the bed, then finally curled up in one corner, her head nestled on his shoulder, grateful for once that she was petite.

This was not exactly the way she'd imagined their reunion, but the steady beat of Mark's heart resounding in her ear as she drifted back to sleep reassured her: their time would come.

And it did.

Lindsay awakened in the still-dark predawn hours to the feather-light touch of Mark's fingers playing over her breasts. It was the touch she had been longing for when he'd arrived and it held all the magic she'd remembered. The contrast of his tanned flesh against the pale silk of her skin excited her almost as much as the touch itself. She tried to remove her mind from her body and impartially observe Mark making love to her, his eyes blazing with the heat of desire, his hands stroking and caressing, seeking all of the tender, sensitive spots that made tiny whimpers of pleasure form in her throat. It was a vision more erotic than any film because of its very gentleness.

Because it was Mark.

Because it was Lindsay.

Then, as his body poised over hers, slick with perspiration, muscles tensed, a gasp of intense pleasure escaped from between moist, parted lips and she welcomed him into her, welcomed him home.

No longer was she able to pretend that she was a casual observer. She was a delighted participant, her body thrilling to each whispered word, each provocative stroke. Just when she thought she was at the edge, her pleasure mounting to an unbearable tension, Mark slowed his rhythmic pace, halted their climb. Then he began it all over again until Lindsay thought she would scream out with frustration, every fiber in her anxious and taut from wanting the shuddering, joyous climax that would carry them away together.

This time, when Mark tried to hold back, she thrust her hips upward, demanding, seeking, determined to find release.

"Please," she pleaded with him urgently. "Please, Mark."

"Did you miss me?" he rasped out breathlessly.

"Yes. Oh, yes," she murmured against his throat, her fingers digging into his back. "I missed you terribly."

"That's what I wanted to hear," he sighed, moving against her more frantically, lifting her hips, his teeth nipping and tugging gently at the tips of her breasts. Sensations coursed through her, sensations that originated in a dozen different ways, from every place his body touched hers, until she was on fire inside and out. She was certain that nothing could top this moment, this feeling, until the next touch ignited something more, something wilder and even more thrilling.

Finally, when she thought she couldn't bear another minute of the exquisite tension, they soared over the top, off on a magnificent journey into a star-filled midnight sky, then glided slowly back to earth on a flight that was like none she had ever taken before.

Eventually Mark rolled over on his back, then drew her into his arms. "Do you have any idea how special you are?"

"I do when you hold me like this," she murmured as he sighed in contentment.

"Mark?"

"Umm."

"What happens now? You said you had a plan."

"Did I say that?" he taunted.

"You did."

"Maybe my plan was just to get you back into my bed."

"We're in *my* bed," she pointed out.

"Same principle."

She glared at him with feigned ferocity. "If that is the extent of your plan, David Mark Channing Morrow, you can haul your butt out of here."

"I love it when you act tough."

"This is no act, mister. Talk fast or move it."

A deep laugh rumbled through the room and he pulled her down on top of him. "Who's going to make me?" he murmured, his lips whispering against hers.

"I am," she replied shakily. It was hard to maintain a suitably tough facade, when what she wanted to be was wildly, wantonly passionate.

"How?"

She held very still, wishing like crazy that her body would stop noticing the very solid muscles on which it was resting. It didn't work. "I was hoping you wouldn't ask that," she admitted.

"I thought so. You're all talk, bright eyes."

"So," she said disdainfully, "are you."

His twinkling eyes met hers. "Okay," he said with an exaggerated sigh. "If it's that important to you, I'll tell you about my plan, though it seems to me there are more interesting things we could be doing."

"Talk."

"Well, I drew up this little agreement."

"An agreement? Like a prenuptial agreement?"

"I suppose you could call it that. I figured you understood all about contracts, so this would be the sensible way to do things."

Lindsay had always thought that, too, but she'd never negotiated one that was so important, so personal.

"What exactly is in this contract of yours?"

"First of all, I was thinking that maybe Los Angeles wouldn't be so bad after all."

"Yes," she said, her heart practically stopping in her chest as she waited for him to go on.

"If you'll marry me—that's clause one, I suppose I could come to Los Angeles part of the year. I guess I can write here as well as I can anywhere else, as long as the smog doesn't seep into my brain cells."

"Are you sure?" she asked tentatively, not yet daring to believe that he meant it. His phrasing had certainly lacked conviction. Then he grinned at her, complete with those heart-tumbling dimples, and her doubts began to fade.

"I'm sure. It's in clause two *a*."

"And I keep my job?"

"Until the children are born. That's two *b*."

"Children?"

"I was thinking of three, but I'm open to negotiations."

"Thank you."

"You're welcome."

"What's in the other clauses?"

"We'll get to those. Are you willing to accept everything so far?"

"If you're absolutely certain, then of course I agree," she said happily. "What made you change your mind?"

"I knew that I couldn't bear to be without you anymore. The last few weeks have been hell. If I have to put up with Los Angeles for part of the year, I'll manage."

"Part of the year?"

"Yes. That's clause three: you'll spend the rest of the year with me in Boulder."

"In winter?" she asked skeptically.

"Maybe not the whole winter. Just for the Christmas holidays," he suggested.

Lindsay regarded him cautiously. She was beginning to think like a lawyer again, instead of a smitten lover. She had a feeling it was probably a very wise transition. "Is that what it says in the contract?"

"Not exactly," he admitted. "Actually, it's a little vague."

"Fix it. Then we might have something to talk about."

"But you will agree to spending Christmas there?"

"Why is that so important to you? Why not sometime in February, maybe Valentine's Day?"

"Because I absolutely refuse to spend Christmas anyplace where there are palm trees, instead of evergreens. You cannot string lights on a palm tree."

"You have a Currier and Ives mentality," she protested.

"What's wrong with that? Haven't you ever wanted to go for a sleigh ride at Christmas?"

"No."

"Make a snowman in the front yard?"

She shivered as she recalled the day they'd spent making their snowman. The snowman had been cute with his crooked little smile. Mark had been amused. She'd been frozen.

"No way," she muttered.

"How about waking up early on Christmas morning, opening your presents in front of a roaring fire and then making love?"

Her eyes sparkled. "Now you're talking my language."

"You like the making love part."

"More and more."

"You won't even notice you're in Boulder," he promised, as his hand drifted low over her abdomen and settled on the sensitive triangle between her thighs. Lindsay moved into that touch.

"Probably not," she said with a satisfied sigh.

"Good. Then pack your bags."

"What for?"

"So we can go to Boulder."

"Now?"

"Christmas is only a few days away. We may as well start the tradition this year."

"You're kidding. It can't be Christmas already."

"Doesn't Trent ever let you look at a calendar?"

"Not if he can help it. We might ask for time off. The weekends tend to get a little blurry that way, too."

"Not this one. You're going to remember every minute, especially the part when you say, 'I do.'"

Lindsay propped herself up on her elbow and gazed straight into Mark's eyes. "Are you suggesting that we get married this weekend?"

"Grace and Jeb are making all the arrangements."

"Oh, they are, are they? Weren't you being just the tiniest bit overconfident?"

"Well, I knew you'd want to give me something for Christmas," he said innocently. "And this is the best present I can think of. What about you?"

Green eyes twinkling like Christmas tree lights, she said softly, "The very best."

Then, with a wicked grin, she added, "Just two things."

"What?"

"Don't you think we ought to sign this contract of yours?"

"Later. What's the second thing?"

"Do you suppose it would be okay, if we did another run-through of Christmas morning? I want to be sure we have it right."

He chuckled. "Oh, we have it right, bright eyes. No one has ever had it better."

"Show me."

"With pleasure."

Much, much later, he murmured in her ear, "Merry Christmas!"

A soft smile tilted Lindsay's lips. It was going to be a terrific Christmas all right. She knew just exactly what to give her mother, too...a ticket to Boulder for the wedding. First-class, of course.

 **Silhouette Desire**

COMING NEXT MONTH

FIT FOR A KING—Diana Palmer
Elissa Dean was exactly who King Roper needed to protect him from
his sister-in-law's advances. The act seemed foolproof... until Elissa's
very presence set King's heart on fire.

DEAR READER—Jennifer Greene
Leslie Stuart needed to teach Sam Pierce, the country's leading
mathematician, to overcome his dyslexia. But could he teach her
to trust in his love?

LOVE IN THE AIR—Nan Ryan
More than the airwaves crackled whenever Sullivan and Kay signed
on at station Q102. But after having left once before, Kay had to
convince Sullivan that her heart was there to stay.

A PLACE TO BELONG—Christine Flynn
Rachel Summers and Eric Johnston needed each other. As a sports
therapist, she had six weeks to bring this pro hockey player back into
tip-top shape—just long enough to fall in love.

STILL WATERS—Leslie Davis Guccione
Another bride for a Branigan brother! You met Drew in
BITTERSWEET HARVEST (Desire #311)—now Ryan Branigan
and his childhood sweetheart reclaim their chance for love.

LADY ICE—Joan Hohl
Cool businesswoman Patricia Lycaster promised herself she'd be
Peter Vanzant's wife in name only. But the more she resisted, the
more determined he was to fan the desire that blazed between them.

AVAILABLE THIS MONTH:

BRIGHT RIVER
Doreen Owens Malek

BETTING MAN
Robin Elliott

COME FLY WITH ME
Sherryl Woods

CHOCOLATE DREAMS
Marie Nicole

GREAT EXPECTATIONS
Amanda Lee

SPELLBOUND
Joyce Thies

ATTRACTIVE, SPACE SAVING BOOK RACK

Display your most prized novels on this handsome and sturdy book rack. The hand-rubbed walnut finish will blend into your library decor with quiet elegance, providing a practical organizer for your favorite hard-or soft-covered books.

Only $9.95

Approximately 16" x 8" when assembled

Assembles in seconds!

To order, rush your name, address and zip code, along with a check or money order for $10.70* ($9.95 plus 75¢ postage and handling) payable to *Silhouette Books*.

Silhouette Books
Book Rack Offer
901 Fuhrmann Blvd.
P.O. Box 1325
Buffalo, NY 14269-1325

Offer not available in Canada.

*New York residents add appropriate sales tax.

BKR-2R

FOUR UNIQUE SERIES
FOR EVERY WOMAN YOU ARE ..

Silhouette Romance

Heartwarming romances that will make you
laugh and cry as they bring you all the wonder
and magic of falling in love.

6 titles
per month

Silhouette Special Edition

Expanded romances written with emotion and
heightened romantic tension to ensure
powerful stories. A rare blend of passion and
dramatic realism.

6 titles
per month

Silhouette Desire

Believable, sensuous, compelling—and
above all, romantic—these stories deliver
the promise of love, the guarantee
of satisfaction.

6 titles
per month

Silhouette Intimate Moments

Love stories that entice; longer, more
sensuous romances filled with adventure,
suspense, glamour and melodrama.

4 titles
per month

Silhouette Romances
not available in retail outlets in Canada

SIL-GEN-1A